UP AND COMING

Molly Parkin was born Molly Thomas in South Wales in 1932. Her first career was as an art teacher and professional painter. She moved on to become the fashion editor of *Nova*, *Harper's Bazaar* and *The Sunday Times*. She now has seven titles available in *Star*: *Love All*, *Up Tight*, *Good Golly Ms Molly*, *Purple Passages*, *Switchback*, *Fast and Loose*, and *Up and Coming*. She is married to artist Patrick Hughes, and they have recently moved from their home in St Ives to spend a year soaking up the inspiration of New York.

D1638191

Also available in *Star*

UP AND COMING

by Molly Parkin

A STAR BOOK
published by
the Paperback Division of
W. H. ALLEN & Co. PLC

A Star Book
Published in 1981
by the Paperback Division of
W. H. Allen & Co. PLC
44 Hill Street, London W1X 8LB

Reprinted 1982
Reprinted 1985
First published in Great Britain
by W. H. Allen, 1980

Printed and bound in Great Britain by
Anchor Brendon Ltd, Tiptree, Essex

ISBN 0 352 30758 7

For my young friends Paul and Christine –
forever up and coming!

Chapter 1

'Someone's wet the bed in number 6!' I announce.

'That vicar and his wife,' Mavis says triumphantly. 'See.'

'He was never a vicar and if she was his wife, well,' our brother Boyo wipes his hands on Mavis's pinafore, 'then you're engaged to be married to Pope Paul.'

Mrs Pugh scowls, scraping the frying pan clear of burnt bacon rind. 'Now then – no sacrilege. Not at this time of the morning, thank you very much.' Blodwen (older sister) comes into the kitchen carrying the last of the dirty dishes from the dining room. 'They've all finished breakfast now. You should be out there,' she says to Mavis. 'Go on, quick! The honeymooners and that Hungarian hiker are both waiting to settle up. Honestly, anyone could walk straight out of this place without paying. We must get more organised about bills.'

'Someone's wet the bed in number 6!' I say it again, preparing to enjoy the sight of poor old Blod getting into one of her states. Hoping that she'll drop the entire tray of dishes to really give herself something to go on about.

'It was that vicar,' Mavis cuts in spitefully. 'The one you fancied so much, Blodwen. Pity you didn't think to ask first if he was a bed-wetter before letting the room.'

'Enuresis – that's the true terminology, if anyone's interested,' Boyo booms out in his rich baritone. The pride of the chapel choir in his time. But currently between professional engagements, waiting to hear whether or not he's got the part of Che Guevara, in the touring company of *Evita*.

'My Elijah took to doing that when he come past his prime. Widdling wherever he was.' Mrs Pugh murmurs tenderly. 'Not his fault, the old love. But plenty's the time that I'd rise with my nightie soaked through to the skin. Yes indeed! Dai Parry, Doctor, do swear my rheumatics took hold on me from then – though, mind you ...'

Blodwen looks as if she'll burst into tears. The muscles around her mouth are working mysteriously, like a mad person grinding her top and bottom teeth together. She's not bad looking, though too refined for my taste – even beautiful in the right light, but today is not one of her good days. I can't help noticing the small lines that have started creasing the corners of her eyes, or the ones which threaten to settle like necklaces around her throat. I hope that when I'm as ancient as thirty-three I'll hold up better. My God – only another sixteen years to go!

'Has it spoiled the mattress?' she asks. There's a break in her voice. 'That's the new mattress, the one in number 6, new in February. I've only just finished off payments.' Silence, broken by Mrs Pugh's, 'Tut-tut, there's a shame.' Everyone's looking at me, as if it were my fault. Things keep backfiring on me these days.

'Christ!' I explode.

'Boadicea,' Mrs Pugh wags her finger at me, 'your poor Mam would turn in her grave. Not to mention your Dadda. I never thought to hear such bad language, not from children of the clergy, but you three ...' She turns from me to Blodwen, who is standing with her back to us all, placing greasy cutlery in the dish-washing machine. 'Blodwen bach, I'm beginning to believe that the bringing up of these three was too big a job for you on your own. It's been a thankless enough task, anyone can see that.'

She is getting into her stride now, warming to the familiar theme, stirring up trouble before catching her bus home. Putting her miserable spoke in. I hate Mrs Pugh. It's a wonder that we ever put up with her, though since Mavis and Boyo left us, it's only me who has her on my back. And I shall be going at the end of the season. Off to university, clearing the hell out of here, leaving Blodwen and Mrs Pugh to run this piddling business on their own. And when it comes to next summer they needn't think that *I'm* coming back to help out. There's Mavis giving up the chance of her odd modelling jobs, her stints as a receptionist or demonstrator, or escort, or whatever it is she does in Bristol. Coming back just to revive her suntan down on the beach, seeing what rubbish she can pick up in her bikini. Pretending she's invaluable at our busiest time, sorting out bookings, saying she's seeing to the annual accounts, planning to pit her cunning against the cold bureaucracy of the Inland Revenue. As if Mavis ever had any sort of a head for figures – except her own 36-22-34. Honestly, if I had to choose between my two sisters as an example for me to mould myself on, I'd be bloody hard put. I really would! One, the selfless Madonna, the suffering martyr of all time. Still setting aside Sunday for chapel at her age, and like as not a virgin as well. Just about as sexless and screwed-up as a cigarette-stub, Blodwen. Mavis as opposite as it's possible to be.

Tarty. I don't like using that word at all. If I heard anyone else doing so to describe a fellow female I'd come down on them like a ton of bricks. It's not a term we feminists allow, belonging with dolly-bird, or cock-teaser, or nymphomaniac. All those sexist terms used by males that we've so come to resent. We had a good debate on it – all the sixthformers in the last week of term, with me in the chair. The headmistress warned us to temper our militancy, me especially. The wanker! She'd be militant, too, if she had sisters like mine, completely unaware of women's liberation. Blodwen I make allowances for – she's too old in the tooth to change now. But Mavis, after all, is only three years older than me. She'll be twenty-one the day after my eighteenth

9

birthday next month, which means that, as per bloody usual, we'll be pooling our parties. A load of bird-brains just like her, with awful Farrah Fawcett-Majors hair-dos. Or whatever's the latest thing. And their crapulous John Travolta look-alike consorts. All business men, mini ones, part-owning boutiques or setting up as estate agents. Roaring about in their pathetic chariots, peppermint-green Cortinas and primrose-yellow Ford Escorts. Nobodies! How I despise them and their limited vision, their plans for the future, their talk of property improvements, ninety per cent mortgages, patio extensions, double-glazing. It occurs to me, listening to them, that their bloody minds must be double-glazed. Allowing no original thought whatsoever to seep through, no mental stimulation, no intellectual enlightenment, no political awareness, no fresh facts relating to the wider world outside. Nothing other than the precise price of a gallon of petrol, or any other of the materialistic trivia you'd expect from such male chauvinist, bourgeois capitalists.

And to my disgust this is the sort of man that Mavis confesses to find irresistible! I blame it on the inadequacy of her education. Not having the brains to secure a place in the local Grammar like me – and Christ knows they take absolute cretins there – she got side-tracked into the Secondary Mod. Hardly the breeding ground for future Bertrand Russells and Gertrude Steins! Rather, the candidates for mass unemployment, for life on Social Security, for enrolment to such Fascist political movements as the National Front. Hopeless existences, existing without hope.

We all saw the danger of this happening to Mavis. Overnight, so it seemed to us, she became unrecognisable. She turned, when she was about fourteen, into a sullen, mindless, but vicious vegetable. I remember because I had just started my periods at eleven whilst she, though older, hadn't even had so much as a glimpse of hers. And then the results of the entrance scholarship came through at about the same time, and meant I'd got through to the Grammar. Perhaps it was jealousy over these two events – she'd always been the centre of attention, being so pretty, and now the limelight

10

was shifting from her momentarily – but I do remember it was about then that she changed.

It was Auntie Gwyneth who came to the rescue. 'This can't go on,' she insisted, shocked by the new Mavis. More aware of the deterioration in our sister's behaviour than Blodwen and I, since she hadn't seen any of us since her previous visit last year. And being Mavis's godmother she felt some responsibility about getting her back on the right tracks again, and this was even without knowing about the big trouble – how Mavis had been caught red-handed stealing a cake from the Co-op. A *cake* of all bloody things! A tart for a tart! That's what I thought at the time, though I didn't say it to Blodwen because I didn't want to upset her more than she was already. In those days I still cared about Blodwen and her moods, the impatience and irritability that she arouses in me now hadn't yet surfaced. Yes, we were still pretty close then, a comfort to each other. Me playing the part of dutiful daughter to her adopted role as the indulgent mother. But everyone has to grow up.

The thing was, about Mavis's tartiness, that I couldn't think of any way to let Blodwen know what everyone was saying about all the boys hanging around our house. Why they were there and what they were after. She lives in such a pure world of her own that she wouldn't have begun to understand what I was on about. I can remember that when Catty had her kittens, it was me who volunteered to clean up the mess, throw away the blood-stained bits of flannel from her box. No-one else in the house wanted to know.

Mrs Pugh declared, in her usual miserable manner, that it was unhealthy for a child my age to display such an interest in these matters. But I'd known about babies and all that stuff for years and years. Wasn't it me who told everyone else at school? Anyone can learn anything if they really want to, it's only a question of reading books. I can still remember my father preaching that from the pulpit, in the dim memory that I have of him. I must have been coming up to my sixth birthday when he died – the first year that Mavis and I did without a party, Blodwen maintaining that it wouldn't

11

look right in the circumstances. She accepted our accusations of 'spoilsport' with silent suffering, her subsequent stoicism must have taken root from then. Drip!

Anyway I never did let on what I knew about Mavis and her boys, never told Blodwen about her having them up in her bedroom and all the things that I used to hear going on the other side of the wall. It got so bad that one afternoon, fed up from shouting to them to shut up with their silly giggling because I was trying to read, I bored a hole through from my side. A spy-hole, just to spite her. I still haven't told anyone yet what I saw.

But I understand now that I'm older with plenty of sexual experience of my own (and no-one in this house has any knowledge of those), that those secret sessions of childish voyeurism must have helped a hell of a lot in the release of my libido. They excited me sufficiently to start exploring my own body. I don't think that I had masturbated before then. The first time that I found my fingers inside my knickers, rubbing myself as hard as I could, it was with a sense of guilt and surprise. They strayed there of their own accord, and stayed to agitate me to a state of dry-mouthed fever. Which swiftly left me, to be replaced by an exhaustion, an infantile trembling of the knees, a feeling that I might vomit. And a strange sorrow such as I'd never known before.

All that from seeing Mavis with her blouse undone and her brassière up around her neck, giggling and squirming whilst one boy did a lot of tickling over her titties. And, as far as I could tell, his friend waited his turn with both hands inside his trousers. Wanking of course, though I don't think I could have realised that then. I knew a lot of things for an eleven-year-old but there was still a long way to go.

But my good fortune didn't last, alas. Not after Auntie Gwyneth came to the rescue. Private schooling was the answer for Mavis. All girls, nice ones from the right background. She'd see to the fees, leave it to her, so we did. And within a month, after a word with the headmistress of the Cymru Day Academy for Young Ladies, Mavis was enrolled as a pupil. Smart new school uniform (no heels higher than

12

flatties) designed specifically to disguise all adolescent curves – but failing dismally in the case of Mavis. She still looked ravishingly fuckable.

I can say that now, though at the time it was as much as I could do to look her in the face, still less acknowledge her desirability. Seeing her in different stages of undress through my peep-hole gave me an uncomfortable feeling in her presence, so that I had started to avoid any occasion where we might be alone together. Besides which she'd taken to treating me as a specially odious pest. Even striking me for no apparent reason whenever she could, ostensibly playfully but still with enough forceful aggression for it to be painful. Christ knows what she'd have done to me had she known I was spying on her! I dismissed the fear of discovery from my mind when it came to me, I was uneasy enough already over the situation, finding it difficult to think about anything else. Unable to concentrate during lessons or whip up any enthusiasm over starting at the Grammar.

'It'll be her periods that's doing it,' I overheard Mrs Pugh confiding to Blodwen. 'Girls do go funny when the old curse come on them. And she's a dark horse, that Boadicea. Always was as a baby, with your Mam ailing all those years. Too clever by half, never good is it really – being bright if you're a girl? Better leaving the old brains to the boys ...'

Mrs Pugh is still whining – when is she not? 'See – the little Madam is not even bothering to listen to us now!' She is frowning in my direction, but the others are barely managing to conceal their mirth. All except Blodwen, who is still loading the dish-washer with her back to us.

'What?' I say. 'Oh! The pissy bed wasn't the vicar's. If you remember, I put that couple in the back bedroom next to the bathroom so that we could accommodate those louts you met in the pub.' I look accusingly at Boyo. He brandishes a tea-towel above his head in acknowledgement, smiling that devastating smile at me. Showing that mouthful of near-perfect teeth, now made even whiter by the contrast of his black curly beard. When he came back this summer, my friend Siriol said that he looked more like Kris Kristofferson than anyone she'd ever seen. Younger, of course, and not so raddled. If he goes on drinking the way he's doing it won't take long – but it does suit him, the beard. And the bastard knows it too.

Shit. It's fabulous being the four-eyed, flat-chested, mousey-haired, spotty-faced, no-bum, pigeon-toed, ugly duckling in this family. I don't want to question the virtue of my dear departed mother, but who in hell was she screwing when I was conceived?! It couldn't have been my father, that's for sure. Otherwise where did the chiselled lips vanish, the splendid sight, the sculptured cheekbones, the light, sparkling eyes set in with sooty fingers and an extra helping of lashes, the abundance of coal-coloured hair? All those advantages that my brother and sisters share in greater and lesser degrees? Where was I when all that was being handed out, that's what I'd like to know? I can only think that the kindliness and devout understanding for which my mother was noted (so they say), must have led her to share her body with some poor sex-starved parishioner – secretly, in the back of the vestry. An intellectual, probably one of the local poets (we Welsh have local poets like the English have local gentry – the buggers are everywhere). Or some spindly academic. Possibly the solicitor who, according to Blodwen, used to live next door to us when we lived in the manse. It would have to be someone reasonably bright to account for my brains. And tall to explain away my legs.

In that respect, and it is the only one, I do have one advantage over my siblings. For although they are much more striking than me, they're none of them blessed with a great length of leg. They aren't short, not in Wales where most people are under the national average of inches. But they hardly stand head and shoulders in a crowd. Whereas I do. It's the sole thing, physically, that I like about myself. Being tall, having the sort of legs that are described as starting under the armpits.

Now I'm working secretly on my nipples, trying to coax

them from these pale, rose-velvet petals with their vulnerable snouts (like those on Catty's new-born kittens), into full-blooded personalities of their own. As pointed as pencils, that's my aim, standing to attention at all times through my tee-shirts. If I can't have cleavage, and it seems I can't – not even going on the pill helped in that respect – then I shall go for straight gristle. Cleavage went out with draggy Elizabeth Taylor anyway. I think that the more exciting erogenous zones are beneath the waistline. Bums are really the thing now. That's always the first bit I look at on boys – and on girls. Maybe because my own bum is such a beauty. 'The cheeks as cheeky as a retroussé nose, Boadicea, my love,' said Zeus Bowen when he pinched them for the first time. And I was only thirteen, but pleased enough at the attention. Though I saw to it that he had to wait another two years before I'd allow him the pleasure of playing with them in the flesh. By that time I'd managed to put myself on the pill (unbeknownst to this lot), and was hell-bent on trying out as many partners as I could manage to cram into non-swotting hours. That was the year that I took my ten 'O' levels, at barely fifteen, the youngest candidate in South Wales. When the results came through, straight A's in all ten subjects, it was in the *Western Star* and *South Wales Today,* with both newspapers carrying the most horrible photograph of me ever taken. Given to them by my headmistress, it was blown up from a group shot of all the school, and I'm wearing my ghastly glasses. I hid every single copy I could find of those newspapers because of that photograph, even going so far as to buying up the remaining copies from the newsagent nearest us. Mere vanity. I resent being type-cast as the bespectacled swot.

Every other member of this family is playing out some rôle. Look at Blodwen, the docile baby, the eager-to-please child, trusting and mature even as a toddler (if the photographs of her hugging an armful of dainty dolls is anything to go by). Hasn't she assumed the responsibilities heaped upon her with no signs of regret, no visible resistance? Wouldn't she accept those same responsibilities all over again if given the alternative of leading her own life amongst strangers in the outside world? Of course she would. It's safer, she has no need to prove herself as an individual. She is simply there to serve us, to smooth the path for Boyo and Mavis and me. Our surrogate mother. And it's only now that she's beginning to question whether the sacrifice has been worth it. I know that she is, though she probably doesn't even realise it fully herself. It's when I go up to Oxford that it will suddenly hit her.

Is a seaside bed-and-breakfast business, however successful at the height of the season and ticking over nicely for the rest of the year, going to be sufficient to satisfy the maternal urges of a thirty-three-year-old spinster? Which is what Blodwen is. A typical nineteenth-century spinster, for all her handsome good looks. Someone out of the Brontës, shuddering away from sex. Oh, if only I could explain sex to her! Jesus Christ knows, I'd pay out of my Post Office Savings for a good fuck for Blodwen if only I could find the right fellow. Unfortunately the Angel Gabriel doesn't come with cock supplied, nor the Holy Ghost. Not any more. Mary Magdalen squeezed the last of the spunk from that source.

And isn't it ironic that here am I, enjoying the libidinous animal urges of my loins? Taking the baby-making instrument into every orifice I own (not my ears, I have particularly delicate ears – and a fear of perforated ear-drums), whilst vowing never, ever to give birth to a child. And there's Blodwen, aching to procreate, but unwilling to face the necessity of fornication. Never mind, we have good old Mavis, Miss Normal to even us out.

Mavis, out of all three of us, will end up with a husband and two children, one of each. And a car of her own, smaller and less expensive than the family saloon – which will probably be a Citröen if her plans work out. A Continental jaunt each year with the children and the French, Italian or Spanish au pair girl. Unless, by then, Asian immigrants are deemed fit enough to care for the fair flowers, the youth, of our country. If there are any Asians allowed into our country by then! Either way, there'll be someone on holiday to see to the kiddies. And to see to the kiddies (similar ages as Mavis's own) belonging to Mavis's pals (similar ages as Mavis and her spouse) who will have taken the next villa to theirs for the same month. So that when the husbands have to whizz back to business at the end of the first fortnight, promising to fly out for that final weekend, the wives will be company for each other.

But they would have found company had they not had their friends in the next villa. No woman without her husband on the Continent in high summer finds herself short of company for very long. Company comes swarming with black, burning eyes. Hot, scalding stares and arrogant overtures. Boys as timid as does, heart-tinglingly beautiful, loiter beseechingly. Handsome young Romeos, with little more than one sexual conquest to their credit, swagger past on offer. Take it or leave it (Señora, say si!). Magnificent machos (ugh!) make brutish advances ... I know all this because I read it in novels and women's magazines. Plenty to choose from if infidelity is on the mind, and knowing Mavis I can't imagine that she'll remain faithful to whoever it is she marries. Not to her first husband anyway. Later, maybe, when she's on husband number three, or four. She's too greedy to ever stop at one of anything.

'Yes, it was one of those louts. Whichever of the three slept in the single bed.' I touch Blodwen on the shoulder. Something dejected about the drooping head must have aroused an uncharacteristic pity in me. 'It's okay, Blod, it didn't go through to the mattress. I took the precaution of putting the plastic covers on that and the double bed when I was making them up last night. Those pigs were as drunk as skunks – I thought there'd be trouble.'

'But cash on the nail – can't be bad!' Boyo says cheerfully. 'Made a full house and that's what we're here for. They pushed off before breakfast so we saved on that, didn't we?' He grins at us all again, especially me, but I am not prepared

17

to allow his irrepressible nature to get the better of me that quickly.

'I should have left the sheets as they were – for you to clear up, Boyo.' I make a distasteful face at him. He saunters towards me, his cock clearly visible in his tight, fashionably threadbare, jeans. But I avert my eyes – it always seems to me indecent, how aware I am of my brother's body.

'You're getting,' he growls sexily, 'too bloody big for your boots.' And before I can escape he's plunged his hand between my legs, grasped me by the seat of my pants and turned me upside down.

'Those two are at it again,' Mavis groans to Blodwen, who's dodging my flailing arms. The guests are impatient to pay up and leave. One of them has ventured timidly through the passage and is knocking on the door of our tiny sitting room just beyond this kitchen.

'Bugger!' I scream, trying to anchor myself to Boyo's legs.

'Shush, shush . . .' bleats Mrs Pugh.

Blodwen remains silent, switching the dish-washer on so that the sounds of the mechanism builds up to drown my rising hysteria. I can't stop laughing. I am convulsed in huge, shuddering gulps of panic and delight. Panic over my precious contact lenses which I feel sure are going to fall out of my eyes in this upside-down position. And delight because, let's face it – brother or not – Boyo is one hundred per cent male. And squirming around in the hard, muscled arms of a healthy twenty-four-year-old at nine o'clock on a nice summer morning can't be all bad. I feel so horny these days!

Then, as unexpectedly as he has pounced upon me, Boyo lets me go. I fall, still giggling, my eyes streaming dangerously but with their lenses intact.

'Oh God!' I splutter on the coconut matting. 'Oh, my God – you bastard! I could have lost my lenses then.' And I lie there in everyone's way, laughing up at him, my legs wide apart, long and thin like an insect's.

My big brother has an incipient erection.

Chapter 2

Mrs Pugh is just finishing off hoovering the stairs and the dining room carpet. Soon everything will be quiet and we shan't see her again until Monday. Good riddance!

'Boadicea,' she says to me, 'be a good girl and empty this contraption for me. It's so heavy with dust I can hardly move it. There's a love.' It was as much as I could do to fight the temptation to let the whole full sack fly in her face and shove it down hard over her miserable head. Grey on grey like a smudged charcoal study. She'd be a great one to caricature, Mrs Pugh. Drawn in the manner of Gerald Scarfe, or the school of Hogarth, so as to include the toned mole skidding low on her chin complete with its full set of grey whiskers.

'I'll do it for you, here,' I say back to her sweetly. 'If you'll just listen out for the telephone, I'm expecting someone to ring.' They've still to get used to the phone ringing for me in this house, as if everyone else has prime wire time. Mavis and her dates, or Boyo and his fast-living friends up in London, or Blodwen and all the complications of her telephone bookings. Those bloody telephone bookings and the trouble they land us into! All because Blodwen went pigheadedly her own way and placed that infernal advertisement

19

in *Wales Away* magazine. On the advice of Owen Evans, Corner Shop, whose fancy piece is working on there as a secretary – the arrangement being an increase in wages for all the advertising she can pull in.

'We don't need it, Blodwen,' I told her after the first cock-up with the phone. There we were waiting for what turned out to be the non-arrival of these three commercial travellers from *Matey Pet Foods,* having already turned away three hopefuls from the door.

'We're not the Hilton,' I explain. She's terribly dense when it suits her. 'In a small set-up like this, with only ten bedrooms, you are always going to have to ask for a deposit in advance. Otherwise you're going to be left with dud bookings like these three Matey sods. What's happened is that they've stopped off for a meal somewhere between here and Cardiff, probably found that they're too tired or drunk to drive on and booked in just anywhere – as they should have done in the first place. We must stick with our regulars and take people at the door with the "Vacancies" sign up – it's worked well enough so far.' By then it was eleven o'clock at night, and these pigs had been due in around nine. In a moment the pubs would be emptying out, a good chance to let off the three single bedrooms that Blodwen was still insisting we kept reserved 'just in case'. The trouble with Christianity is that it doesn't mix well with business, there's too much bollocks about having given one's word.

'But what happens,' Blodwen had bleated, 'if we let the rooms go now and then these three chaps turn up? It'll do our reputation no good at all ...'

'Blod,' I'd spoken firmly, 'just leave it to me. Go on to bed now, you look just about all in.' She'd started her periods that morning. I happened to know because of the Tampax tube floating about in the back lav. Unless it was Mrs Pugh's – I'd laughed cruelly at the thought.

And so she had gone to bed, leaving me in charge. As soon as the 'Land of Song' public house had emptied on the corner, I put the porch light on to draw attention to the 'Vacancies' sign which I popped out there at the very last minute. It wasn't as if I hadn't given the Matey trio their chance to show up at the final count. I let their rooms to three Australian schoolteachers who hadn't been able to face the prospect of a night beneath canvas in the stormy conditions which had suddenly sprung up. The Matey lot arrived at eight minutes past midnight.

I was unable to recommend an alternative place to stay, the Australians had already told me what difficulty they'd had finding anywhere. The bad weather had driven many campers to seek indoor shelter. As I explained patiently to these three cunts.

'Great, sonny!' The burliest, a Scotsman, had barked. This happened a lot in the middle of the night, people taking me for a boy. I preferred it that way, it made for less trouble, especially with boozers. My choice of pyjamas and striped dressing-gown was no accident. Nor was the heavy torch that I had in my hand. 'Self-protection,' I'd joke if the latecomers looked friendly. I always opened the door with it held at the ready. Now I turned it so that it should catch the light, just in case one of these three hadn't noticed it.

One of them coughed. 'We should have rung, Jock. We should have, to say we'd be late.' He shuffled his feet around his black briefcase. Full of sick-making samples for shitty pets, no doubt. I don't approve of dumb animals in our house. And now I had three of them taking refuge on our doorstep.

'You should have,' I said. 'We hung on long enough. But after midnight the booking no longer stands. It's another day, you see.'

All three of them stared at me, blinking uncomprehendingly. 'The Hotel and Catering Act of '58. I've a copy here if you'd like to check.' I made as if to move from the door, convincingly enough, though my feet stayed exactly where they were. There was no such document of reference in the house, any more than there had been a Hotel and Catering Act in 1958. But this was the sort of bilge that would impress these thick blockheads. It was cold and I wanted to get back to my bed, back to Hirschfeld's *Sexual*

Anomalies and Perversions, Zeus Bowen's copy, which he has promised to give me for my birthday.

The third one spoke, the best-looking of the three (I'm not slow to notice these things, however awkward the situation).

'You are meaning to say,' he said slowly, consulting his watch, 'that if we had arrived nine minutes ago, at one minute to midnight, our rooms would legally still have been ours?'

Clever bugger. But not as clever as me. 'They would indeed, sir. And were still at that time. I only let them go five minutes before your arrival here. Listen.' I opened the door fractionally wider. 'The cistern is still in use.' Sounds of the top lavatory being flushed could be heard. The top floor was where we put honeymooners and young couples if we possibly could. They were up and at it all night long. Poking and pissing.

The coughing twerp coughed again, a chest in need of attention. 'You've nothing then? Nothing at all to offer us? Not even a sofa?' The wind howled around the bay, driving a sheet of heavy rain before it. All three instinctively turned up their collars. Fools!

'Not really.' We were always being asked that when people were desperate. Of course, we did have sofas and suchlike. We had as many as four makeshift places for pals to put their heads down. And at that time of the year between Easter and Whitsun, before Boyo and Mavis had come down for the season, we had their two bedrooms going free.

The good-looker lit a cigarette, offering me one first. I said no, I didn't smoke, not that kind anyway. He laughed so that I should understand that he knew I wasn't simply referring to the brand. It was the laugh that made me change my mind.

'On the other hand, if two of you don't mind sharing,' I looked at the barking Scotsman and the coughing twerp, who nodded eagerly, 'I might be able to fit you in somewhere.'

'And me?'

That wasn't necessary, Handsome. We both know that you

22

know that I'm no boy. 'I'll find a corner for you.' In my bed. 'Trouble is that we're not going to be able to cope with your breakfasts. Best thing is to settle up the bill now and push off first thing. You'll find plenty of cafés open early, especially near the motorway. It's all I can offer you.'

'Champion, Sonny.' The Scotsman belched a thick sarcastic sound.

'Shove it, Jock,' his cautious companion muttered, stifling another cough, 'the lad's only trying to be helpful. Anything's fine by us.' He turned back to me. 'Look, kid, here's the cash now. Enough to cover any inconvenience we've caused.' I could tell without counting that it was way over the odds.

'Fine then, just follow me. And easy on the noise. All our other guests will be asleep by now.' I led them up the stairs. The tasty one I left waiting for me in the hall.

It is whilst I am emptying the hoover onto a sheet of the previous day's newspaper, that I think I hear the telephone ring. But I could have imagined it because my attention has been drawn both to a glimmer of gold midst the dry drifts of dust, and towards a small item of interest which I must have missed reading the day before. The glimmer of gold turns out to be, disappointingly, merely half of a small safety-pin, instead of the piece of priceless jewellery that I fantasise about finding. Not that our clientele are exactly the Concorde Crowd (the latest term, so I read, for the Jet Set). We haven't had Jackie Onassis pass through our portals yet – but now and again they do come, people with plenty of pounds to spare.

'They're not short of a few bob, that couple in number 9.' I come down into the kitchen and say when I've done the rooms. 'Neither's that old bird on her own. You should see her shoes. And her silver. Fancy travelling around with a caseful of that stuff – probably nicked it from all the hotels she's been staying in. We'd better get our good knives and forks under lock and key.'

But nobody appreciates my idea of a joke. Only Boyo,

when he's around. Poor old Blodwen, and naturally Mrs Pugh, and to a certain extent Mavis, regard our paying guests with something bordering on reverence. As if our tiny hotel were some sort of fucking holy of holies and the visitors were divine worshippers. It's an attitude I despise, that genteel subservience, a fawning eagerness to be treated as an inferior. I find it grotesque when Blodwen starts stammering, almost speechless when she feels that she may have given offence. Or when Mrs Pugh, caught with pinafore on and duster in hand, genuflects before some perfectly ordinary man and his wife as they pass her in the passage. And Mavis, whatever would Mavis have been like with those Matey chaps that night? She wouldn't have slept with Young Tasty, that's for sure. She would have considered what I did with him pretty outrageous. Mavis never mixes business with pleasure. That's what she always says, but what she really means, I know, is 'don't shit on your own doorstep'. Mavis has changed a lot since she went to Bristol.

I empty the dry, smelly dust into the dustbin outside the kitchen door in the sunny back-yard. Later on in the day I will come into this small, secluded space and lie naked all by myself. Let the rest of the world flee to the shore with their transistor radios, their blithering dogs, their blathering beach games and their bawling kids. I see them when I stand at our front windows doing the rooms. I even go out onto the verandah sometimes with my binoculars to study humanity at its worst. Lolling on lilos, licking their ice-cream, bronzing their biceps, bulging out of their obscene beach-wear. Mavis amongst them.

But never Boyo. Boyo disappears when the sun comes, he's off with his pals. God knows where they go – the rest of us have never been invited. But Boyo is bound to be different, not just being the only boy in the family, but having spent so much of his childhood away at school. There are and always will be whole chunks of him that we'll never know about, things that happened to him during those years, friends that he made then that we'll never meet. And I understand that more than the others. People should have their own

24

secrets. It's been difficult for me to have any in this household, but I've managed. It only needs a little thought and some imagination. So I never pry into what Boyo does and who he does it with. But we're getting closer and closer, as the rest of them have noticed. Soon he'll start telling me things.

Having shaken the dust from this page of the newspaper I now read the short item that had caught my attention. I study the paragraph with interest: ALL THE NICE GIRLS DIAL A SAILOR, it says. Then it goes on to describe an admirable scheme which has been launched in Devon in which nice families are invited to dial a Dartmouth number and ask to take out one of the 100 foreign naval officers being trained at the Royal Naval College there. Just to make these foreign lads feel less homesick. The scheme is labelled Operation Meet-a-Midshipman, and although the authorities acknowledge that it might 'attract undesirables', it is a risk that they are prepared to take. They have no objection to single girls ringing up to invite the men out. The average age of these foreign officers is between 18 and 25 – too young for Blodwen, I reflect irritably. And in any case, Dartmouth is too far away. Now if such a scheme were to be launched in Cardiff it might make more sense. Not that Blodwen has ever shown any interest in younger men. Nor, for such a nice girl, any particular love for sailors. It is time to discuss the problem of Blodwen with Boyo and Mavis, I decide. If I don't get something organised, nobody will. She'll be left the way she is going, a dusty old maid on the shelf. Ever-present on the consciences of the rest of us.

'I've done your hoover, Mrs Pugh.' I shout through from the kitchen. The decision to do something about Blodwen has lightened my spirits. All I need now is the expected telephone call and the world will seem rather a cheerful place. My disposition is never other than optimistic, it's just that at times I'm more impatient to leave this nest and its cloying inhabitants than at others. Today is one of those days.

Mrs Pugh swears that the telephone hasn't rung, and I scowl distrustfully.

'Don't look at me now in that silly way, Boadicea. Wouldn't I say if it had?'

Not necessarily. Mrs Pugh is afraid of the telephone and will do anything rather than answer it. She thinks that it's electric and that you can get electric shocks from it. She even refuses to touch the electric alarm clock. It's almost as much as she can bring herself to do, to turn on her own television set. But the delights of the small screen are sufficient incentive to dare taking the risk. A strange voice at the end of a telephone line is not.

But now she's gone home, thank God, and I'm on my own, still waiting for the call to come. Zeus Bowen returned from America late last night. I need to be told how he spent his entire poetry tour thinking about me. I find, to my surprise, that I've missed the old bugger more than I expected to. Yet three months sounded nothing when he told me he was going.

'You'll probably die out there, killed by kindness, like Dylan Thomas,' I'd spoken flippantly.

He'd buried his bearded face in between my bare legs, biting sorrowfully on my sparse pubic hair as if it were dainty mustard and cress, which it resembles. What I'd really like in the way of a bush is a big one like a busby, the same as Mavis has. So that I'd have to go to Gwen, Beautician, in the High Street and have a wonderful wax depilation before wearing my bikini. Mavis moans about having to fork out the six quid, but I'd rather be forced into that position than put up with this babyish fluff that I have.

But Zeus is enchanted by it. 'How otherwise,' he always rhapsodises, 'would I be able to see so clearly your exquisite labiae, the adorable curve of your mound of Venus, this delicate separation ...' And he sighs and starts chewing. As he chewed the day he told me of the poetry lecture circuit in the States. I made a mental note to remind him to wash his face before going home to his wife, and to borrow my toothbrush and clean his teeth. One of the hazards of ultra-fine public hair such as mine is that it can become trapped between the teeth without a person even being

26

aware of it. A solitary pubic hair is chillingly recognisable when seen away from its natural setting.

'Oh, Boadicea, Boadicea, I wish you could come with me! How will I endure three months without seeing you, when after a week I start losing my mind with the longing?'

His despair was genuine, within seconds I fould feel his tears, slippery upon my skin. I had felt them before many times, over my breasts, inside my thighs, beneath my buttocks. There wasn't a spare inch of my body which hadn't at some time or other been drenched with Zeus Bowen's tears. They were, so he'd claim, an outward expression of his internal ecstasy. A poetic sentimentality to which Zeus Bowen is prone, a quality for which he is alternately praised or decried, depending on the critic. It was sure to heap him with accolades in the U.S.A. He must be the closest anyone could find to their idea, everyone's idea, of the Celtic bard. The booming, sonorous voice, stirringly seductive in its huskiness. The unruly curls. The passionate eyes, the pouting, sensual mouth. The swift changes of expression from exhilarated and childlike delight, to those of utter desolation. And though I am, and will continue to be emotionally involved with this very precious man, I can see that he is a parody of a Welsh poet. He even goes so far as to inhabit the same shape as Dylan Thomas, dimpled and dumpy. But I don't mind that a bit, nor (once to my bitterness, though not any more – I have conquered my jealousy) do other females. Especially not his wife, that poor, deluded, pathetic creature. Talk about our Blodwen being ancient – Mrs Dilys Bowen must be forty-five if a day. Must be!

Siriol, my friend, was working it out that Zeus Bowen is thirty-four now, as it says in his Faber and Faber anthology, and he married when he was seventeen. Right, well, she was his schoolteacher. Which means that she must have been at least about twenty-four, seven years older than him, *then*! I say *then* because as we grow older, it's said that the female of the species shows signs of ageing faster than the male. It's not a fact that feminists like me choose to propound. I would question the theory myself, feeling it to be the result of male, rather than female, research. But looking at the decaying wreck of Mrs Dilys Bowen, I fear there may be a lurking truth in it. I pray that death may strike before I ever reach that state!

Siriol knows nothing of my love affair with Zeus Bowen. She would slaughter me if she did. She has worshipped him, with the rest of the Girls' Grammar (including the staff), from the day he started his poetry readings at school. I remember how envious they were that I knew him, that he'd been a friend of the family for so many years. My father's protegé, in fact. It was my father who had first recognised his poetic talents. My parents would have been proud of his progress since then. In Wales he is regarded with the same pride as Lloyd George, Aneurin Bevan, Dylan Thomas and Richard Burton – especially since he has chosen to remain here amongst his roots.

Siriol would kill me if she knew. Nobody knows except Zeus Bowen and myself. And that is the way it will always be.

But I couldn't answer his beseeching groans. What could I say to accompanying him to America? My mouth was full, the reply would have to be postponed. While Zeus Bowen was delicately grazing my pubic crop I was practising my burgeoning talent for deep-throat. Having conquered the gagging as the cock skimmed my tonsils I was training myself to take spunk with the same ease as swallowing food. If only the fucking stuff was as tasteless as they claimed! Who put that out in the first place, I'd like to know? Some old girl whose taste-buds had atrophied obviously! It was expecting total tastelessness that caused me to vomit so embarrassingly at my spunk-swallowing debut. If I'd known the flavour was that of sucking the slime from an over-used face flannel (one that had done special service on private parts), and with much the same texture, then I should have been better prepared.

So, instead of answering, I stretched my skinny arms further round his thick thighs and started tickling his arsehole with the tips of my fingers. In a short while, when I judged him to be just about ready to come, I would introduce my little finger right into his hole. Slowly, the way he'd taught me to do. And then having opened it up, I would exchange that finger for a larger one, then two. The way he does, or rather *did*, with my cunt when we first started doing these things together. When I was fourteen, and first agreed to take my knickers down.

I've come to like this probing about in people's botties. It's amazing how few males have had it done to them before. That Matey guy for instance. He was a married man, yet when I whispered to him, 'Tell me all the things that your wife does to you and I'll see if I can do better,' I found that he had never indulged in anal foreplay. Hadn't even entered his mind that she'd enjoy it – or that he would. He was awfully conventional, mind. Straight missionary style and off to sleep if he'd had his way. With some ideas that the back of the body was solely the province of 'queers' as he called them. I soon put him right.

'Come on – bugger me, you'll like it!' I sprang up on all fours and shone the bedside lamp on my beautiful bum, so that he'd see his way in. 'It's all right, don't be frightened. There's no shit inside – my alimentary tract is quite clear of traffic this time of night.'

You'd have thought he'd known that sort of thing dealing in dog food. But few of these commercial travellers have even got 'O' levels. If I charged extra to the paying guests that I've educated in my bed, I wouldn't have needed to apply for a grant to go to Oxford. I'd be able to keep myself in luxury for the next five academic years. Oh yes, I intend being a student for easily as long as that. My Ph.D. and all that sort of thing. I believe a Prime Minister should have this scholastic background, especially a woman. Margaret Thatcher isn't a fool.

'Will you be faithful to me in America, Zeus?' I cruelly extracted his cock from my mouth just as he was on the point of coming. The index and middle fingers, of my right hand, were doing a delicate tango up his arse-hole (they are very *slim* fingers). Whilst my other hand played billiards with his balls. Both balls were already in the bag, it was just fun constantly rearranging their order with my thumb as cue. Zeus had declared himself to be absolutely transported, but in such strange, strangled tones that I knew his desire was mingled with the deep-rooted fear that I might do him a devastating injury. Which I never would, unless driven to it. In which case I might. He understands my capacity for cruelty.

'Faithful! Bloody faithful? To you, Boadicea? When have I not been – answer me that?'

His voice reached a crescendo, ending in soulful agony. I popped his pulsating penis back into my mouth, preparing to toss back the steaming sperm-cocktail like the sophisticate that I've become. He'd be faithful all right, however long he was away. The love Zeus Bowen felt for me transcended all mundane lusts. I was his Muse, his inspiration, his entire reason for living.

Now I am in the big front bedroom of the middle floor of our B. & B. waiting dolefully for his call. It's three months since the declaration of his passion. And although in that time I have been unconditionally accepted for Oxford, life is nevertheless flat.

It isn't as if I have gone short on sex. Few days pass by without me having a fuck somewhere. With my usual care. The screws that I choose are strictly with married men, persons with a social position to maintain, boys who belong exclusively to their girl-friends, fiancés just on the brink of getting married. Even bridegrooms – yes, really! Yesterday I had Lloyd Parry, who was getting married to Glenis, my friend Siriol's sister. We did it quickly in the garage at the back of Siriol's house after the ceremony. We were both drunk, making eyes even in the chapel waiting for the bride to appear. And I had meant to sample Lloyd ages ago but never got around to it. He said the same, that he'd always thought of me as something special, but had been warned off by other people who said I never gave it away. He was con-

vinced that I was a virgin – even after we had done it!
How dumb can you get!

'Your first infidelity, Lloyd,' I said brutally. 'And you
only married two hours.' He didn't like that. He protested,
'I love you, Boadicea. I've fallen in love with you. Now.
Here. I have. I don't have to go on honeymoon with Glenis.
I can tell her. She'll understand – it was only to Swansea. We
weren't going far . . .'

'Sure,' I said. 'Tell her – it'll be good for a laugh.'

He stared at me. 'You didn't mean it – just now?' And
he gestured in the direction of our genitals, his open flies and
the damp gusset of my knickers.

'I mean it – don't be so daft!' I gave him an affectionate
shove. Men are more vulnerable than me over casual sex,
they're more romantic about one-night stands, promising to
ring or to get in touch again. I mean, who wants to re-
sample the goods? Once a thirst has been slaked with several
short snifters, or one lengthy quaff, there is no compulsion
to drain that particular barrel dry. There are too many other
different drinks on the shelves. It's more thrilling to try
other tastes.

I'm not representative in these matters, I have only myself
to go by. Siriol, who has a painful track record, says that all
boys are bastards. They get what they want and then shove
off to the next girl, leaving you high and dry, your reputation
in tatters and rags. I tell her why bother, why bother with
boys? Get on to real men. But she shudders at that.

'The only man I'd bother with, Bo, wouldn't bother with
me.' Then we fall silent for our different reasons. The man
she refers to is mine. Zeus Bowen.

But Siriol, like everyone else, believes that I haven't actually
done it yet. She says to me, 'Perhaps, Bo, yours is the best
way. Getting on with your school work, using these years
for study. Then latching on to someone smashing up at Oxford, the brightest of all. Making a brilliant marriage – okay,
I know, you're never going to get married – but honestly, in
my opinion, sex isn't what it's cracked up to be. I think my
mother is right when she says that they had more fun be-

31

fore the permissive age. Our lot have had too much of it too soon. I read that yesterday in the newspaper.'

'You read the wrong papers,' I say to her sternly. Other than that I make no comment.

I wonder, as I gaze out the window waiting for Zeus to ring, what Siriol would say about me screwing her new brother-in-law. There is little love lost between her sister and herself, so she wouldn't be indignant on that count. I doubt if she would believe it of me. She'd believe it of him, she'd jump at the chance to condemn him as a bastard like all other males. Just because he's popped his prick in my pussy. Siriol over-reacts. In any case, the news is never going to leak out. Lloyd the lucky bridegroom is hardly going to let on! And why should I? I have no need to boost my super-healthy ego by bragging about my sexual conquests. There's nothing easier than inducing erections, the mistake that people make is in confusing this mini phenomenon with emotional and intellectual commitment. My commitment to Zeus Bowen has little to do with sex; I accept that his to me has more to do with it. I can't imagine how he has managed for three months without me. And since we haven't been able to correspond with each other, because of the complications and the fear of discovery, it must have been unbearable for the old love.

The telephone remains silent. On the other side of the road, the beach is beginning to fill up. There is no parking space free, the space in front of our house is more than occupied by the American Chevrolet with the Dallas registration, belonging to the American family whose room I should be attending to. I turn to view the chaos: the double bed in the centre stripped of its sheets and blankets, one pillow at the bottom edge and the other on the floor beneath it; the single divan alongside in a similar state, and the toddler's cot. What's up with this family? Is it an American custom for parents to indulge in a free-for-all with their small children through the nocturnal hours? Incestuous pillow-fights?

Yet the brats, though American, look docile. Even, if you're into all that stuff with small children (which I've never been), adorable. The boy, crew-cut like the father, has big, chocolate-drop eyes and a cute mouth with no lips. Just a little line like a cartoon drawing of a child. And the tiny girl is the same, her shape distorted by the bulk of her nappy in her frilled nylon knickers. Just like a baby-doll, except when you prod her she doesn't cry, just wriggles and wrinkles up her button nose and begins to laugh.

The mother is Welsh, but not a local girl, not from hereabouts. Her parents retired to a bungalow, one of those that the older residents of the place sneer at as being jerry-built, at the back of the dunes. This is the first time the grandparents have seen their grandchildren. The grandmother has terminal cancer, with less than six months to live.

I know these facts because I've made it my business to read all the letters and documents that they leave strewn over the room. Each morning – they have been staying with us a week already with another one more to go – it's my laborious task to restore some kind of order in here. The first day, after they had made their extraordinarily flamboyant departure from the street in the pink, pearly-sheen Chevrolet, I called Mrs Pugh, Blodwen, Mavis and Boyo from the kitchen to bear witness to the state of the room for themselves. So that I shouldn't be accused of exaggeration. None of us had ever seen anything like it.

I'm not normal when it comes to tidiness, mind. I wouldn't agree with the rest when they accuse me of having an obsession with neatness and everything in its place. But I admit to a certain fastidiousness, a need for harmony in my surroundings. I am a great one for economy and system and method. I see muddle as evidence of mental confusion and actually enjoy sorting out other people's mess and muddle. So I make a magnificent chamber-maid.

Today, I find the task somewhat daunting. Last night I agreed to baby-sit for these children whilst their parents went out for a meal with the old folks. When I agreed, I had only just learned of the grandmother's cancer and was eager to help towards banking another happy memory of times spent together before the old lady's death. Yet another nugget to console the children's mother back in Dallas. What a charm-

33

ing girl, they'd say of me, to baby-sit that evening so that we could dine out with mother on one of the last occasions – that's what I really relished. But when the time came I was sorry that I'd committed myself. Siriol and several of the guests from her sister's wedding were going on to Shingles, the new disco near Penarth, and wanted me to go with them. The sexy encounter with Lloyd had whet my appetite for more. Just as well I was baby-sitting. I haven't left this small town yet – no reason to fuck up the respectable reputation I've built so carefully all these years. Besides, I comforted myself, tomorrow Zeus Bowen would be back.

The American kids were no trouble at all. Twice I looked in and both of them were sleeping soundly. The third time, an hour later, the little girl Cindy had turned herself over and lay with her face buried deep in the pillow. I'd enquired of her mother whether it wouldn't be wiser to dispense with that pillow. In all the books that I've read about baby-care, a pillow for such a young child is not something they recommend. But the mother said it was fine, that Cindy had always slept with one. Ignorant slut. I removed the pillow, placing it outside the cot. If any child was going to die, I didn't want it to be on my time. I had a future to think of, a brilliant career ahead of me. No point taking chances now and fouling it up. I always apply this kind of logic to such situations. Like not crossing the road at a dangerous junction, or refusing lifts from people whom I know to be reckless drivers. I'm taking a definite hand in my own fate, by being this cautious. Whether or not it will work remains to be seen. I could be struck dead tomorrow, despite all the planning and care. I could, more to the point, develop some incurable species of venereal disease. There are alarmist medical reports being issued all the time relating to sexually-transmitted viruses which are becoming immune to antibiotics, and are sweeping the country in epidemic proportions. But I pay little attention to such scare-mongering tactics, feeling them to be based on the puritan ethic that the promiscuous should be punished for the pleasures they so freely indulge in – the emphasis being on the free. Why do moralists insist that pleasure should be paid for? Because they enjoy little pleasure themselves, except the delight in delivering words of warning.

Siriol caught a mild dose of the pox the term before last. We worked it out that it must have been from the foreign exchange student who was billeted in her house, though I had reservations about this myself. I'd had him too (on the final night – so that he'd have no chance to spread the word around) and had got off scot-free. It was a close shave, thinking about it afterwards. Because even if he hadn't given it to her, she – if she caught it from someone else – could have given it to him ... who in turn could have given it to me ... then I could have passed it on to Zeus ... there it would have ended though. Because Zeus Bowen doesn't fuck anyone else, not even his wife. He's sworn on the Bible that he doesn't do that. Poor Dilys, no wonder she looks so woebegone. A classic case of sexual frustration. Not that she needs to take the risk of any more children. In my view, four is four too many children for any one man to have to support. Especially a poet. The last thing a poet needs is financial pressure and the mundane worries of a family. Look at Dylan Thomas! And any number of artists through the years whose output has suffered from having a wife around his neck, and a brood of babies. Who was it who said, quite correctly, that the pram in the hall was more to blame for the unwritten novel and the unpainted canvas, than any amount of wine, women and song?

All Zeus Bowen needs is a mistress like me. Someone with an intellectual sensibility to match his own, an individualist who will match him in his individualism. As much of a celebrity as himself – which is what I shall become.

But I haven't told him that. I don't think that his ego could accept it yet. He still clings to chauvinist values as far as women are concerned. I think that secretly he likes the thought of Dilys back home at the hearth seeing to his children, treating him as a child to be simply kept well-fed and warm. She couldn't have always been so thick, she started off as his schoolteacher, after all. Not that the teaching profession can boast many enlightened individuals on the feminist front. And certainly not when Dilys Bowen was still teaching. We're sadly short on research as to what went on in the Ark.

I start gathering up the children's clothes from the carpet, American tee-shirts emblazoned with cartoon characters. The only one that I recognise is Snoopy, but now I find a canary-yellow, striped satin wind-cheater with Kermit the Muppet, moping on the pocket. Jesus only knows how often in one day these American kids, Cindy and Hank, get changed! However many tiny garments I recover from the floor and fold back into the drawers (few are soiled enough to even warrant washing), more keep coming. I can't think where from, unless these vast canvas hold-alls have secret panels.

Today I have promised to take a whole pile of the family's clothing to the laundromat. The father was imploring her to ask me, since he's running out of drip-dry shirts, suits and socks. I have never seen him, or her for that matter, wearing the same outfit more than once. And it isn't even as if their bodies are dirty! Each morning and evening all four of them get bathed. Mrs Pugh is absolutely scandalised. She says that we should tell them of the terrible water-shortages that Great Britain has suffered these last few summers. How the officials on Cardiff County Council were making pleas on the television and local radio for ratepayers to think twice before boiling a kettle for a cup of tea – let alone running the taps full-on for a bath.

'In our house we were taking it in turns,' she whined indignantly, 'as to who should get into the bathwater first. One bathful of water for five people, no less!'

'Ugh!' I muttered under my breath. But her eagle ears caught it – she has a hearing apparatus as acute as the original Marconi set. Picks up anything.

'Ugh, indeed! Ugh? Boadicea, it's a good job that your namesake didn't display the self-interest that seems to have overtaken you in recent times, my girl. Patriotism was alive as fire in her veins, and she has stood as an example to the British race, an historical inspiration to us all, Boadicea!

36

And it was for patriotism and the doing of our duty, for the communal good of the country in its hour of need – the need for water – that the six of us shared that bath-water in the last drought.'

'You said five, Mrs Pugh.' I stared at her blankly, with more than my usual insolence. It was my silent way of shouting, 'Bollocks!' Now she was really cross, she never liked to be picked up on any point.

'Five! Six! What difference does it make, my girl! It's the principle we're discussing here. To my mind it doesn't seem right for these Yanks to come over here on a holiday and commandeer our precious water supplies. By August, who's to know what state the farmers will be in – crying out for the stuff, the fields parched as the desert ...' Mrs Pugh collapsed on a kitchen chair, clutching her throat. Carried away by the force of her own rhetoric. She would have made an effective lay-preacher, but the Welsh haven't allowed women into their pulpits yet. By the time I have any power in Parliament there probably will be few pulpits left, I've already worked that one out. Support for female lay-preachers is pretty low' on my agenda. But it's as well to note these minority groups, such a minor issue could prove a mighty potent vote-puller. It shows one's interests to be compassionate and wide-ranging, no cause (however fucking cranky) being unworthy of interested concern.

Having collected and sorted out every item of children's clothing, placing Cindy's on one pile and Hank's on another, I now tackle the father's. His name is Elmer, Elmer Roosevelt. No connection with the former President of the United States. As far as I can make out from various documents, including his passport, Elmer Roosevelt was born in 1945 – the same year as Zeus Bowen – and states his occupation as 'engineer'. Which could mean anything. My guess is that they're just a suburban couple in Dallas. The wife, maiden name Barbara Jones (Elmer calls her Barbie), has merely exchanged nationalities rather than backgrounds. She is very like the sort of girl-friends that Mavis gets on so well with. Vapid, but well-groomed. Her mouth gummed up with lipgloss, her polished cheeks gleaming with glowing creme-rouge until they resemble shiny red apples perched arbitrarily between temple and nostril. On certain days I notice that the cheeks of these girls occur as low as the lip-line, stretching over to the ear-lobes. On other occasions the mode is no cheeks at all, simply a gash of grey shadow to emphasise the skeletal structure beneath. Worn with a liberal application of dark mascara, the fibrous variety that tends to moult, so that to my amusement their entire maquillage (as they call it) can be ruined by a single blink. Inky fibres descending like a swift shower of soot upon the poreless surfaces of their smooth skin.

But men like these girls. They like them a lot. Not the sort of men that I admire, not ones like Zeus, but I'd be willing to bet that the Matey guy has a wife at home exactly like this Barbie Roosevelt. Interchangeable zombies, false finger-nails and all.

I pick up one of Barbie Roosevelt's finger-nails from the floor, three more of them like flower-petals have fluttered from the bed-side table. But there are several still lurking in the bed. It was after one-thirty this morning when these two returned from their night out. They had gone on to the Conservative Club after dinner for more drinks – they'd no need to tell me what they'd gone on for. Four sheets to the wind, as Mrs Pugh would have said. They could have entered a contest with Boyo – walk down this white line without wavering – and lost. If anything Barbie Roosevelt was worse than her husband, though he was staggering and buckling badly at the knees. She could only manage to crawl on all fours up the stairs.

I laughed with him obligingly as we hauled her up the last few steps, and even offered to help undress her for him. I've had to do plenty of that in my time here – Blodwen gets off lightly needing to retire to bed as early as she does. But my offer was graciously refused. As I left the room where we'd managed to deposit her on the double bed, I watched Elmer Roosevelt getting down to the job in hand with obvious relish. It made me wonder what on earth it must be like, being screwed and sleeping with the same person every night of your life. I can't imagine me doing it, not in a million years. I'm never ever getting married.

Half an hour later I heard Boyo coming in with the ones he'd picked up in the pub (one of which piddled the bed). They'd been drunk enough when he'd booked their room earlier on in the evening. Oh well ... I gave a fleeting thought to Lloyd Parry and Siriol's sister, Glenis, on the first night of their honeymoon. A plentiful foreskin, Lloyd's, like a thick shawl ...

For the first time ever I dreamed that Zeus Bowen had proposed to me – as if I'd say yes if he did!

Chapter 3

Boyo is driving Mavis and me to the Cash & Carry. Yesterday passed with no call from Zeus Bowen. I am numb with something more than mere disappointment, I feel waves of nausea alternating with bouts of vitriolic resentment and a shameful urge to burst into tears. Even now, at this very moment, I am trying to dispel a painfully thick lump in my throat. Swallowing so rapidly that my eyes have filled up, I scrabble furtively in the pocket of my old mac, the one I feel really satisfyingly shabby in (suiting today's mood very well). But there is no hanky. I rub my eyes roughly with the sleeve instead. Boyo, in the driving seat by my side, darts a glance in my direction.

'You okay there, kid?' His voice is so full of kindly concern that something in my chest heaves over, the lump re-forms in my neck. I merely nod mechanically, like a toy animal that car-owners sport in their rear windows.

'Looks to me as if she's sickening for something,' Mavis butts in brutally from the back seat. 'Love, I shouldn't be surprised. It's about time, I must say. By your age I'd been engaged to be married at least twice.'

'I'm a slow developer,' I managed to mutter in a gruff voice. It only needs Mavis's abrasive flippancy to dispel my maudlin sentimentality.

'You can say that again!' Boyo playfully pings my nearest nipple, the car swerves violently towards the kerb.

'Careful!' Mavis is laboriously painting her fingernails, a hot lush pink to match a new lipstick she's wearing. She speaks as if she has food in her mouth to avoid besmirching her front teeth with the colour. Usually it's easy to tell where Mavis has been because she leaves this disgusting trail of crumpled tissues in her wake. Each of them stained with whatever muck she's wearing on her mouth that day. The sordid end-result of a prolonged process of blotting. But this morning we have been in too much of a rush for these niceties.

We have to be back to serve lunches today. The start of the new regime, the switch over from Bed and Breakfast to the daunting B. & B. and Full Board. Blodwen hung the sign out this morning, though we will be almost full when today's arrivals come. I've changed all the beds, double and single, in each of the ten bedrooms. Including those of the Roosevelts, although they're staying on. Today, being Saturday, is our busiest day. Even Mavis mucks in and pulls her deliciously-distributed weight. She helped me do the laundry, exaggeratedly wrinkling her nose at the stench of the dried urine donated by Boyo's pal. I took pleasure in forcing her to help me fold it up along with the others. Christ only knows how she'll manage when she has children. Although she drools so embarrassingly over little Cindy and Hank, she doesn't want to know when it comes to dirty 'diapers'. When Barbie uninhibitedly waves what appears to be a richly filled chocolate sponge around in the air, Mavis gasps 'Pooh!' and beats a dainty retreat. Whilst I sensibly offer to dispose of the same.

I am becoming indispensable to the Roosevelts. They are already talking jokingly of taking me back with them to the States. Cindy cries each time they leave to go out in the morning because I'm not going with them. This surprises me, I always thought small children could tell instinctively when people liked them or not. And I don't like Cindy, or Hank for that matter. They're trivial and boring. I don't need their

41

gurglings to reassure me as to my own identity. I know that I exist. I'm not like Barbie Roosevelt, barely capable of functioning except as a wife and mother (I absolutely *curdle* when I hear her wheedling around her husband for spending money!). Nor would I be like her if I ever had the misfortune to find myself in her position. Making such a palaver over the simple matter of bringing up two children – and whatever kind of a mess must they live in back home if she can't even cope with one room here?

There is no real reason why I should be going to the Cash & Carry with Boyo and Mavis. They could manage just as well on their own with the bulk-buying. But Boyo is only really interested in stocking up on cut-price booze, and Blodwen doesn't trust Mavis to choose the right breakfast cereals (last summer we were stuck with a gross of Shredded Wheat), or even the simplest household cleaning things. Mrs Pugh refuses to clean with anything other than her usual brands and claims them to be the cause of the mysterious skin complaints that she suffers from now and again. In short, Mavis is becoming rather more of a liability as the seasons progress. Hardly any real help any more, since I've grown up to be so much more capable. Still, never mind, I shan't be here next year to let it get on my nerves. It'll be a kibbutz holiday for me then – I've already written away for the details.

No, my real reason for accompanying them is to have a serious talk about Blodwen. Apart from liking to have everything settled about her future before I depart in the autumn, I am now more than a little concerned about the state of her mental health. I'll be interested to know if either of the other two have noticed how abstracted Blodwen has become of late. How tense and irritable, withdrawn and pale. Like a Victorian heroine with the vapours. Only worse.

Last night I came upon her in tears as she was laying the tables in the dining room for breakfast. Her face, when it turned towards mine, wore an expression of positive suffering. She was looking as I felt after not hearing from Zeus Bowen. The last time she'd looked like that was at our father's funeral when they lowered the coffin into the earth. And only the

42

afternoon before when, creeping quickly past the front room where the corpse was in residence, I had caught a glimpse of that same expression on her face as she had emerged from the room. She spent long sessions on her own with my father's dead body, such that Mrs Pugh had begun to mutter that it was morbid. It was years later before I understood the meaning of this word 'morbid'. When I did, I remembered my older sister's odd behaviour at the time of the death in the house. I would have been more inclined to describe it as unhinged.

I think she's a little bit unhinged now. 'Do you think,' I say to Boyo and Mavis, 'that Blodwen is going just a bit barmy?' My question is perfectly serious. But they both of them burst out laughing. Mavis especially. 'There's only one barmy one in this family.' She says it meaningfully, making a silly pointing finger towards her own forehead and another pointing to mine. She means me.

'Do you suppose it's sexual frustration?' I continue, ignoring Mavis's stupidity. 'I feel we should do something about getting her serviced.' May as well get straight to the point.

'Boadicea!' Mavis sounds shocked now. I've noticed an increasing streak of bourgeois puritanism in her these days.

'What?' I turn to stare at her, experiencing the usual stab of surprise at how ravishingly pretty she is. The suntan that she's been slaving to achieve has now ripened to a biscuity-bronze, so that her blazing eyes seem more violet than ever. She is growing her hair again, which she does with no trouble (unlike me), and I see that already it is well beneath her shoulders. At one time I had been able to boast to the other girls in my school that I had a sister whose hair was so long she could sit on it. It was true, too. Sometimes she would allow me to play with it. I'd sit there for hours on end plaiting it in braids, loving the weight of it, the luxury of all those curls. Burying my face in the fragrant cloud with my eyes shut tight, praying that one day I'd wake up with my own hair looking the same. Instead of the straight mousey growth that I'm stuck with. It's only lately that I've taken to lightening the tone. Meant as a nice surprise for Zeus

Bowen's return. When he went away I hadn't got my contact lenses either. He'll be coming back to quite a passable-looking blonde, who even gets whistled at in the streets – at a distance.

But whatever improvements I manage in my appearance, I shall never be able to compete with Mavis. Hers are film-star looks, everyone says so. I can't for the life of me imagine why she has decided to bury herself in Bristol, of all dumps. If I looked like her I'd see to it that my face and my figure would make my fortune, live off my looks in the big time. I'd go to London and sign up with a proper modelling agency, or try and break into television, or do something in films. But Mavis is lacking in ambition, she doesn't seem to be able to set her sights on anything. Tragic really. The result of second-rate, mundane mental equipment. She has the drive and determination of a sea anemone. I wonder if she's as useless in bed?

None of this detracts from the pleasure of looking at her. I'm not in the least surprised that all her admirers dote on her. But even in that department she doesn't use her marbles. You'd think that a girl like her would be showered with gifts – cars, clothes, fur coats, expensive jewellery, exotic trips to glamorous places. But not a bit of it. She's very choosy as to who she goes out with. Sugar daddies don't stand a chance. Nor do Asians, Africans, Arabs, Chinese, Japanese and Europeans. Except the French, they're all right because of their sexy accents. Sacha Distel is Mavis's idea of a 'dishy' man. *Sacha Distel!* That fawning frog.

No-one over the age of thirty appeals to her either. Thirty is the watershed in her mind between youth and old age. She really believes that at twenty she is almost past it – whatever *it* is – that she's missed the boat. She and her ghastly friends spend hours bemoaning their ages, peering into their compact mirrors, their constant companions, in the eternal search for the dreaded sight of a wrinkle. In that way I'm lucky, though I shudder at the obscenity of Dilys Bowen's withering. I'm not afraid of growing old. I shall age more elegantly than Mavis. Lean and leggy as I am. Mavis could easily

44

deteriorate into obesity, become florid and overblown. After all, look at what's happened to Elizabeth Taylor.

But that's a long way away, years and years in the future. Mavis is probably in her prime, at the peak of feminine desirability. I wonder if Boyo would like to fuck her? When he and I get closer I must make a point of asking him. He doesn't suffer from Mavis's prudishness, he'll give me an honest answer. Now he is seriously considering my proposal to find some cock for Blodwen.

'You thing that our dear, devoted sister needs screwing?'

'Boyo!' Mavis is bleating again. We both ignore her.

'I do, Boyo. Don't you?'

He doesn't answer immediately. We have arrived at the Cash & Carry and he is concentrating on steering the car into a narrow parking space between a large lorry and a white Citroën. I anticipate Mavis's comment, and it comes without fail.

'Ooh, lovely car!'

I look at Boyo's brown hands on the steering wheel, the scattering of black hairs over the back of them. They are very masculine hands, like everything about him. Physical. I have begun to wish that Boyo wasn't my brother, so that I might sample his body myself. My eyes slide over him, over the unzipped, short, black leather jacket which emphasises the width of his tremendous shoulders, over the brilliant blue of the shirt that so cunningly matches his eyes, down to the controversial black leather trousers. The ones which so delight me, and so dismay Blodwen and Mrs Pugh. I can tell just by looking at their faces when he has them on. Mavis openly voices her disapproval: 'Obscene.' Well, they are a bit obscene, but that's what I like. 'Pays to advertise, darling!' had been his chortling rejoinder, and I agree with him. A person who certainly knows what Boyo has on offer. A giant cucumber and two big round oranges.

I unclip my safety belt as he switches the engine off. He unclips his and twists around in his seat to face me. The soft leather clothing squeaks seductively as he does so, and I am granted the pleasurable view of his entire crotch in this new position. Black, shiny and forbiddenly sinful.

'It's not as if Blod's really old, not in actual age,' I persist, not willing to let things drop now. 'She only seems old to us because we think of her as a mother.'

'Over thirty,' Mavis heaves a heavy sigh. 'Harder to get decent guys interested in any chick over thirty.'

'Don't be so shallow, Mavis, for Christ's sake!' I turn a scathing snarl towards her. She has lifted her cloud of curls up away from her neck and is balancing it beautifully on the top of her head. The action raises her pointed breasts, darkening the velvet depths of the cleavage. Mavis always manages to show cleavage, whatever the time of day. This morning, despite the overcast skies and forecast of showers, she is wearing a patterned purple and pink blouse with capped sleeves and high padded shoulders. The neckline is slashed wide in what is known as a sweetheart style, very popular for pin-up photographs during the last war. Around her neck she has, borrowed from my bauble box without asking, a string of clear pink glass beads. They match the pink of the tight pencil-skirt, slit enticingly to permit the wearer to walk. Though how anyone can walk in Mavis's shoes I shall never know. She claims to need this ridiculous heel to elevate her height. That if she doesn't teeter around on a minimum of five inches, she'll look short and fat. It isn't true. But I think, to my satisfaction, that it may be because of me that she's self-conscious about being petite. The difference between a chihuahua and a greyhound. Or a cute kitten and a baby giraffe. Nobody is ever satisfied with themselves. I know I'd rather be a pocket Venus than me, in spite of the pride I profess in my legs.

She shrugs, paying scant attention to my scorn, more interested in her reflection in the rear-view mirror. I don't think that Mavis is going to be very much help over Blodwen and her sex-starved old pussy. Perhaps our brother has more social conscience towards the spinster in our midst.

'What do you think, Boyo?' I lift my legs coltishly and rest my feet against the dashboard. My old Burberry mackintosh and the thin skirt beneath slide back from my bare

46

thighs almost to my knickers. I am aware of Boyo's eyes travelling the length of me, from my flat, childish sandals right up to where I've deliberately chosen to clasp my hands under each cheek of my bottom. 'Boyo?'

He drags his attention back up to my face. 'Boadicea.' His eyes are warm and amused (hell – he's attractive!) as he stretches to pull my mackintosh down over my knees. 'Can't have the natives stampeding,' he says, indicating two twerps with deliveries who are gawping in through the windscreen. Then he continues, 'Blodwen – you feel we should dust her down and rescue her from the shelf?'

I nod. 'Don't you?'

'Well now,' he turns away and gazes out through the window. 'In my opinion it's up to the individual concerned.'

'Oh, don't come all that!' I explode. 'Look, we're not talking about Human Rights. This isn't a meeting of the United Nations. In my view our sister could do with a bit of dick. Tom's dick, Dick's dick or Harry's dick – it doesn't matter. I'd just like to see a smile on her woebegone chops for a change. Lately she's been looking as if she'd like to do herself in. Haven't either of your two noticed – or are you too fucking preoccupied with yourselves and how easy it is to get your own end away?' The ferocity of my attack surprises even me. I find two pairs of violet orbs piercing through me. Mavis speaks first.

'Hold on, Bo,' she says, hesitantly for her. 'You'll get your turn, you know, all in good time.'

'Yeah, kid,' Boyo adds. 'You little sex-pot, you've got everything going for you. Honestly, this time home I've been really amazed at the transformation.'

'Sure thing,' Mavis agrees eagerly. 'Now with these lenses and blonde streaks – you look really great. Geraint Thomas (one of her louts, with a Lotus Elan, who works in his father's estate agents' office) was saying so only last week. He said to me, "Mavis, that kid sister of yours is growing up into a piece of hot stuff, a really tasty crumpet. I'd like to take a bite, I can tell you for nothing!" That's what he said – no word of a lie. And Barbie Roosevelt said what she

47

wouldn't give for your legs – Elmer had remarked on them to her. Elmer has always been a leg man.' Mavis looks triumphant.

I feel my heart sinking. They both think I am talking about me. That I've simply brought up the subject of Blodwen to air my own grievances because life isn't giving me my share of the spoils. Indignation rises hot and raw in my throat that they should assume if that were the case I would simply sit back and let it happen. As if I am as undemanding and gutless about opportunities as they are themselves. Even Boyo, content to take understudy rôles and second leads in provincial touring companies instead of the cream which belongs to him. They are each as dumb as the other, charming and beautiful, sexy and decorative, but both about as thick as elephant shit.

'You're both as thick as shit.' There. I've said it, now I'm waiting to be clipped about the head by one of them, torn off a strip, put back in my place. But do they? Do they fuck! They pat me on the shoulder in a patronising manner, the pretty patronising the plain. I give up. I'll find poor old Blod a bit of cock, something to comfort her, even if I do have to do it on my own.

Chapter 4

Zeus Bowen is back! I bump into Dilys and three of her brats in Davis the Dairy. I'd gone to get yoghurt, she was in there ordering extra milk.

'There's Boadicea, there's Boadicea!' The six-year-old twins clamour for my attention. They're not bad boys, I suppose, but I harbour a terrible jealousy towards all Zeus Bowen's offspring. Towards anyone who can legitimately claim even a shred of his loyalty and love. And he does love his children, even if he doesn't love their mother. The eight-year-old girl smiles shyly behind her spectacles. Her ten-year-old sister doesn't appear to be with the rest of the brood. She's the one that I know best, the one who was still invariably awake whenever I've baby-sat in the past. Not that I've baby-sat for some years, pleading pressure of school-work as an excuse. When the real reason was that I suffered qualms of conscience over screwing their father. Even now I find it difficult to greet Dilys with the same ease with which I hail everyone else. Pity creates barriers between people.

'Hello, Boadicea.' I steel myself to look at the lined face, the long-suffering smile, the lustreless eyes. Though I don't feel myself to be the direct cause of this pathetic creature's unhappiness, not wholly responsible for the breakdown of her marriage, I am involved. She is not aware of it, but I have had to listen to endless tirades against her inadequacy. I know her much more intimately than she knows me.

'We haven't had a chance to congratulate you yet,' she says, 'on winning your scholarship to Oxford. Balliol College too, isn't it? Well done!' She is smiling a thin cerebral smile at me, there is colour in her cheeks. And her hair, which is normally in a straggly, disorderly bun at the back of her neck, looks somehow different. She has had it cut in a vaguely fashionable shape so that it hangs to her earlobes, turning under at the ends, like smooth little curtains. Even the grey in it looks as if it's deliberate.

I feel sick. I know before she mentions his name that her husband has returned from America and that her confidence and appearance is linked to that.

'I intended to write and tell Zeus, I knew he'd be so pleased for you, but then I thought that I'd wait and save up all the nice news for his return.' The eight-year-old is tugging at her sleeve, whilst the twins seem to be wreaking havoc amongst the biscuit display near the door. Davis the Dairy is ready to serve me.

'Four plain yoghurts, please Mr Davis.' My mouth feels as if it's frozen. But I can't stop myself from making certain. 'He's back is he, Mrs Bowen?'

She turns, surprised. 'Oh, didn't you know? He's been out and about today – I thought he'd called at your house this morning. Yes, he came back yesterday. Now then, twins ...' She turns to go.

'Anything else for you, Boadicea?'

'Nothing that I can think of, Mr Davis.' Nothing except this poor bitch's husband, these brats' loving father, served naked as nature intended into my bed ...

'Nice to see you, Mrs Bowen.' I walk jauntily from the shop. He must have called at our house when I was in the Cash & Carry with Boyo and Mavis.

'Lovely to see you, Boadicea. Good luck up at Oxford if I don't see you before – I'll tell Zeus to call in.'

'Yes.' I smile at the children. Tell him by all means, give

him permission to screw his arse off.

As I open and shut the door I hear Mrs Davis the Dairy, come in from the back room.

'Well, indeed,' I hear her exclaim, 'was that young Boadicea Jones? There's getting to be a smart girl she is!'

Twice as smart as you think, dumbshits!

Chapter 5

Mavis and I are waitressing this evening, whilst Blodwen and Boyo make the dinner. Boyo is the best cook in this family, he has a special way with food. Most of it's wasted on our clientèle, since, much of his despair, he has to cut down on the garlic. He'd put garlic in the custard if Blodwen would let him. Not that Boyo would serve custard on his menu, to many people's disappointment, although there is a great call for it from middle-aged Northerners, especially men. Boyo prefers cream, soured, which Davis the Dairy has to order specially for him. Or else he likes to use yoghurt. He claims these products to be more beneficial, more health-giving. Boyo is on the edge of becoming wholly vegetarian. He cooks meat with something bordering on disdain.

Tonight there is discord in the kitchen. Blodwen has refused to allow Boyo to serve nut cutlets as a main course to families who have been travelling all day. They have been arguing over the nutritional value of such a dish, compared to roast lamb, gravy, potatoes and two veg. She is allowing him to make curried ratatouille tomorrow evening. I shall switch duties with her if she keeps to the promise, and she can have a try at serving these outlandish meals. Holiday-makers seem to think that we waitresses have hides like elephants. There is no limit to the insults I have to put up with.

Even Mavis, with her winning ways and navel-deep cleavage, has to take a full share of the ribaldry.

'Since when do you folk, you guest-house proprietors think it's all right to serve one sliced grape for starters?' this purple-veined turd said to me ten minutes ago.

'Sir?' I stand smiling at him, the halved grapefruit still in my hand, ready to stuff up his horse-nostrils at another word. His wife is at his side, eager to back him up. But that's all right too, the water jug is at her elbow, just within my tipping distance. There is a silence in the dining room. This couple have never stayed with us before but many of the others are regulars. They will spring to my defence at the lift of an eyebrow.

'I'm referring to the size of that thing – do they shrink them at the Customs when they're being smuggled into South Wales?' Turd smirks all around, waiting for some English support. His gross wife giggles at his elbow, their bravado is a combination of Guinness and genial release of high spirits because they've managed a week off work together. I know that. The put-upon proletariat, poor fuckers.

'Now then – manners!' A Welsh voice near the window sounds threateningly calm.

'Oh, Taff's taking exception to my little joke!' Turd turns around mockingly.

I'm usually ready to take on anything. If I were a writer I might find a confrontation between these two somewhat amusing, even going so far as to encourage such an event with a cunningly murmured comment. But not today, nor any day in this dining room. Not when it means that I would be the one stuck with doing all the clearing up after such a fracas.

'Would you prefer tomato juice, sir?' I ask beguilingly. 'There is a choice. You and your wife are a little late for dinner, otherwise you might have realised.'

The rest of the dining room regard me with great respect. Mavis would have flounced off long before this. She is eager to be off and away on the dot tonight. Saturday night for her

53

means a tour of the fashionable pubs along the coast, three watering-holes, in a fast car with her friends. A meal at around eleven, then into the Gwalia Country Club (Conservative naturally), to drink and dance until two in the morning. Christ only knows when she manages to fit in any sex. I think sex is pretty low down on her priorities.

I have no plans for the evening, but my pores are perspiring at the expectation of pleasure. Blodwen has confirmed that Zeus Bowen did call at the house this morning, quite casually, as if it was completely unimportant. Which it is for her.

'Diluted, is it?' Turd's weary joke continues.

'The tomato juice, sir? I could arrange for it to be diluted if your digestion is too delicate to take it neat.'

People titter at nearby tables. I bend politely from the waist, knowing perfectly well that this way the people behind me are getting a good view of my bum. I'm wearing tantalisingly brief shorts which barely cover my buttocks, and a frilly apron in front. Blodwen doesn't approve of this attire, nor does she think that Mavis's boob-tube is suitable for serving food. But Blodwen is too nervous to verbalise (an odious Americanism of Barbie Roosevelt's that I'm trying out for size) her misgivings. Blodwen is more edgy than I have known her in my entire life. I must put my inspirational energies into finding a solution. One thing is certain – none of this week's guests will turn up trumps in that respect.

This isn't always the case. Sometimes it is possible to conduct a small romance on the side, beside serving three meals a day. Last summer, for instance, there were more opportunities than one to get Blodwen laid. Plenty to go round. Apart from having one of the concessions from the Cove Pleasure Camp for visiting comedians and performing artistes (who point blank refuse to stay overnight at the Camp), we had all the influx from the Welsh Nationalist Rally which was taking place locally. In addition there were the two sporting events – the big mid-summer cricket match, and the Welsh Golf Trophy. And, of course, we had the Poetry Festival, with Zeus as the leading light.

Thinking back, I only wish that I'd put my mind to the problem of Blodwen then. I can remember numerous likely lays for her, more than one of them single – either divorced, or a widower. People become single earlier than they used to. Two of the widowers that I'm thinking of were under forty, one whose wife had been killed in a car accident (on the way back from her yoga class – an exceptionally calm corpse). And the other a victim of anorexia nervosa ('I didn't miss her till she'd gone – she faded away before my very eyes').

I am well aware of the problem of Blodwen herself. There seems no desire whatsoever on her part to get embroiled with any male, under or over fucking forty. Married, divorced or a widower. The thought occurs that perhaps she's a lesbian ...

'How's it going in there, kid?' Boyo's shirt is unbuttoned to the waist. This kitchen and its ventilation need re-designing.

'It's going fine,' I say truthfully. 'Everyone's saying what lovely meat it is. I've told them it's Vale of Glamorgan, that always pleases them.'

'It's New Zealand actually. Deep-frozen, Cash & Carry,' Mavis interrupts, glancing at her watch.

'I know what it is,' I answer irritably.

'Here's the pudding, you two. Load up the trays.' Blodwen's jaw is clamped hard together.

'Looks lovely, Blod,' I say. ' The first day of full board has been a great success so far. Another year in the bag.' Blodwen understands and appreciates this sort of talk. I know how to soothe her. Her face relaxes, and she runs a limp hand over her pale forehead.

'Thank God.' She says it with a great depth of feeling. For the first time it occurs to me that even she might be fed up to the back teeth with this shitty business – just as much as I am. Mavis and Boyo don't want to give up this couple of months of escaping down here. Free bed and board, pooled pocket money out of the takings. A comparatively leisurely working life, evenings free from eight o'clock onwards. That's the advantage of catering mainly for family folk and straightforward provincials: they eat early. What they call the evening meal starts promptly at six-thirty, by public demand. If they had their way we'd be serving them 'supper' too – small snacks like cheese and biscuits or pieces of cake, with drinks of cocoa or Horlicks at around nine-thirty. That's when they wend their way up 'the wooden hill' to 'Bedfordshire'. The clichés come pouring forth, coy euphemisms about retiring for the night. The shyness that full-grown adults, most of them mothers and fathers in their time, display about the simple function of taking their clothes off and going to bed continues to astound me.

It's because they are afraid that you'll think that when they're going to bed together they are going to fuck. This is seldom the case, I have to report sadly. I should know, I'm the one scouring the sheets in the morning for signs of it. Seminal stains are surprisingly rare in our house – I would have thought there would be more of it going on between people when they're on their hols. But no. Perhaps they're intimidated by the strange beds or the fear that someone in the next bedroom will hear them going full-pelt at the mattress. The families who come away with their small children sharing the same bedroom are understandably inhibited – though not the Roosevelts. It would be interesting in later years to question little Cindy and Hank as to whether they were aware of their parents' nocturnal fornication. At the start of the Roosevelts' visit I'd had to change the sheets as many as three times a week, not to mention the towels! That was because Barbie had her period and was humping like a rat, regardless, through it all. The scene looked like a set-piece from a Peckinpah movie! But there was no apology, no attempt to hide the evidence from the children. They might have been forgiven for believing their father to be a mass murderer neglecting to wash his hands after an evening at his favourite pursuit. Or their mother to be a virgin, nightly deflowered again and again (having tacked the tear together between bouts).

Honeymooners are a different kettle of fishy fingers. There I can't complain of sexual inactivity, though it is irritating the way that many of the brides like to save me the bother of making the bed in the morning. They have made it themselves. Embarrassed by the evidence of their freshly acquired marital bliss. On one occasion, ripping back the neat arrangement of bedding belonging to a pair from Bolton who'd hardly been able to keep their hands off each other on arrival, I counted as many as seven separate splodges of milkiness (holding the sheet to the light of the window to be absolutely certain that I wasn't mistaken)! Yes, seven. Seven times, they must have done it. (Unless they were writhing and leaking all over the place from just the once.) And yet neither of them looked as though they had enough spunk in them to fill a fountain pen. You can't judge an engine by the chassis.

Nor, just because there's snow on the roof, has the fire necessarily gone out in the boiler. There was this geriatric, white-haired old codger, who knocked at the door and booked a room for the night last Easter. When he came back he had rather a motherly fifty-year-oldish woman with him. To judge by the excessive politeness between them she was no wife. Their sheet could have challenged any honeymooners'.

I'm interested in these things, keenly interested, as I am in all aspects of human nature. It will be cheering for this nation to have as their Prime Minister someone who is capable of encompassing sexuality without false modesty or bourgeois embarrassment. I shall abolish censorship immediately I assume power, on the first evening, if I can fit it in before dining at Number Ten. And I shall choose as the men in my Cabinet chaps renowned for their cockmanship. And the women in it will be clever cunts like me, who are keen on cunnilingus, so that we'll be able to trade tasty telephone numbers between us. I've never claimed to be against an anarchic abuse of power.

'You're daydreaming, Boadicea – jump to it – pass the puds through.' Boyo is touching me tenderly on the cheek with a fiercely bunched knuckle, looking at me quizzically with his light eyes. There is love in them. I blush, to my annoyance. He keeps catching me like this, unprepared for the onslaught of his gentler side. The tray is heavy, but I see that Mavis has already left with hers. She is ahead of me in the passage-way, her figure outlined against the streaming early evening light from the open front door. If I were a fella I'd fuck it.

I loathe that word 'fella', it's one of Mavis's. She had a whole clutch of these verbal abominations. 'Lady' is another. She introduces me to dross that haven't met me before as being a very 'brainy lady'. It drives me 'up the wall'. But I don't want to 'get into doing a heavy number' about it. The trouble is that I feel so strongly about her speech that I don't trust myself to speak of it, for fear of 'giving offence'. And it's only since she went to Bristol, before that she spoke just like me, normally and with a straightforward Welsh accent. What she does now with her vowels sends goose-pimples over my scalp. She's doing it now, as she enters the dining room with Boyo's baked apples and yoghurt. She's affecting some alien twang of her own with predominantly English overtones. As if she's ashamed of the Welsh in her voice.

I follow dourly, like the hen backing up the bloody peacock, and bash my tray down as close as I can to the purple-veined turd. Then I give him and his wife the smallest portions that I can find. They are going to complain over the yoghurt. And I agree with them, baked apples and custard is much nicer. It reminds me of life with my mother, though I can't have any memory of her serving it to me.

'How's the yoghurt going down with them?' Blodwen asks anxiously on our return to the kitchen. Mavis malevolently displays her full tray to Boyo.

'No takers,' she says with unjustified triumph. '"Anything else on offer?" That's what I'm being asked. Something edible like strawberries and cream, or ice-cream with hot chocolate sauce, or jam tart with custard, or chocolate gateaux.'

Our brother curses viciously, quietly so that we can't catch what he's saying. Blodwen tut-tuts and begins to busy herself opening tinned peaches with the electric tin-opener, following this with cans of evaporated milk from the store in the refrigerator. Nobody bothers to ask me how I've got on.

'Nobody bothers to ask me how I got on,' I say casually. My own tray is completely clear. Boyo looks up, his brooding expression clears at the sight of the empty tray in my hands. We exchange conspiratorial smiles, just he and I.

'I simply plonked them down in front of the swine. No nonsense, that's the way to do it, Mavis.' I say. But it's water off a duck's back. Mavis is studying her watch again and smoothing her eyebrows with a spittle-tipped forefinger.

'Yes, well, if you're so smart, kid, you can take over my tables too. Is that okay, Blod? There's nothing much left to do now, just these and the coffees. And if I don't get a move on doing my face I'm going to be late when they all come to call.'

I am speechless at her selfishness yet again. But it is pointless to complain, I know from past experience. It's just easier to let her go.

'Is that all right with you, Boadicea?' Blodwen asks fearfully, dreading a scene between us.

'Yeah, sure,' I say off-handedly. 'Leave little old Cinders to do all the work. But mark my words – I'll be the one to come home with the prince.'

They all look at me strangely, no-one saying a word. I've embarrassed them into a self-conscious silence, and though this pleases me, I can't see why it is I have managed to produce this reaction. Is it because they are reminded that I am growing up at long last? That I may share their sexual ambitions, their romantic longings? Poor suckers. If only they knew.

'And what dalliance have you got lined up for yourself this evening, little darling?' I stroke the back of Boyo's neck in a flirtatious manner, aware of Blodwen's frowning disapproval.

'Anyone left in the dining room, Boadicea?' she asks, though I've already announced not more than five minutes ago that the whole set of duffers are now esconced in the tiny television lounge.

'Not a soul, Blod', I answer her obligingly. Then I slide my entire arm around Boyo's strong neck, coaxingly, and whisper so that Blodwen can easily hear me. 'Can I come with you tonight, to wherever you're going, Boyo? Will you take me?' And I stare at his curved lips, knowing perfectly well that he'll say, 'No, it's not the sort of thing that little girls like you should be exposed to!' Just as he has always said in the past. But this time there's a difference. Instead of gazing up at him as I would once have had to do, I find for the first time that our mouths are on a par, our lips are on a level. Even, dare I say it, that his are slightly below mine. That's how much I've grown up. And the fact has not escaped my handsome brother either, another difference.

'Well,' he says slowly, holding me to his shoulder and starting to squeeze me until I'm gasping for breath. 'Why not, for a change. It might do her some good, Blodwen – give the kid a taste of life.'

He looks enquiringly at our older sister as if asking permission of a parent. But the situation in this house has gone beyond that. As Blodwen very well knows, I do as I wish these days. And she knows she can trust me to behave as she would wish, with restraint and a maturity beyond my years – as I've made it my business to have her believe. Poor old bitch. But now it's started to pay dividends, this caution and cunning. There are never the questions that Siriol has to put up with from her mother, for instance. No, 'And where do you think you're off to at this hour of the night?' if ever I should decide to take a midnight walk along the shore. I could come in at dawn, which I frequently have after hours of passion with Zeus Bowen, and no-one would be waiting up with a scolding. Why should they? I'm a responsible young person, my religious sister has set me a fine example.

But now she's demurring, not altogether with conviction, she just needs to be reassured. That's all.

My own heart is crushed, hard up against my brother's. My lungs are emptied, I have no breath left. Despite this sadistic hold, my spirits are spiralling. I'm to be allowed out with Boyo. At last I shall be joining his world. Who was interested in whether or not my older sister agreed?

Chapter 6

'I really thought that you weren't going to be let out, young lady.' Boyo has to shout over his shoulder to be heard, the zoom of this motorbike drowns out the rest of the world. It's a borrowed machine, a powerful American monster, lent by a friend who has three of them. It's the first that I knew about Boyo and motorbikes, I wasn't aware that he could even ride one. Certainly it's my maiden-run, I haven't ridden pillion before, Siriol will shit herself with envy.

I'm scared stiff, we're going at some speed it seems to me. But when I screamed this into Boyo's ear, hanging on for dear life as we cut through motorway traffic to overtake a thundering lorry and so avoid an oncoming car, he simply shook his head and laughed. I'm sure that he can't have heard what I was saying. And I don't bother to reply to his words now. Conversation will have to wait until both of us are standing on terra firma – if that ever takes place again.

He hasn't confided where we're going, it's to be a surprise. But we're heading in the direction of Cardiff, a city unfamiliar enough to be immensely exciting. I have only been there four or five times in my entire life, travel having been neglected in my development. And those excursions were conducted under my own initiative, being connected with my research into adequate contraceptive measures. Widespread travel of the world, that wider world outside Wales, is something that I have yet to experience. With Oxford, my life will begin. But I don't want to think about that now, I am reserving it for the future and I'm not even looking forward to it. I don't allow myself any of the spiralling excitement that my schoolfriends share in contemplation of their new lives now that we've left schooldays behind. At this minute I'm thinking about the here and now, about whether I'm to survive this hair-raising journey and tell the tale. If it were not my brother in charge of my life, I would have refused this ride. My chances of running this country are under considerable threat. But do I care? I don't give a toss – what is gratified political ambition compared to this? A night on sophisticated tiles with the sexiest-looking man that I know ...

I tighten my hold on his stomach and swallow hard to keep my last meal down as we swerve past heaven's portals one more time, to a clear stretch of road ahead. When we stop, twenty minutes later, my eyes are still shut and my arms are still clenched. I fear that if I let go I shall fall to the floor. Boyo tenderly disengages me, holding me for support all the while.

'L-l-ook at that,' I struggle to gain some control over my stammering gums. The lower half of my jaw feels as if it has emerged from several bouts with a heavyweight boxer. But it's my knees that I'm now preoccupied with, each is jitterbugging quite independently of the other. Dancing to completely different rhythms.

Boyo only laughs, gathering me into his arms, removing both my helmet and his at the same time.

'Save the jiving for inside,' he says, 'they've got real music here.'

I cling on close like a child, feeling more like a lover. I hope that a passing couple think I'm his girl-friend. I wish I was wearing high heels and girlie clothes, like Mavis wears, instead of these unisex white denim jeans. The only thing to commend them is their tightness, clean on tonight straight from the wash so that they fit like a second skin. Snaky and lean with no pantie-line to mar the outline – I am wearing no panties. Above this, in an act of daring, I have on the white boob-tube that Barbie Roosevelt bought and discarded this week as being too small for her. 'Here honey,' she'd said to me in her effusive American odiousness, 'Any good? If not, chuck it.' But I hadn't chucked it, though it patently wasn't my sort of thing, not at all. Little did I dream that the opportunity to wear it would have presented itself quite so soon. Neither Boyo or Blodwen have any idea that I'm wearing such a thing, so skimpy and revealing. On top I have a boyish white bomber jacket in tough cotton to match the lower half of me. 'That'll do fine, kid.' That's what Boyo had said when I'd presented myself. 'It's no great shakes sartorially. Just a casual spot where we meet for a drink and a bit of a knees-up.' He was saying that to reassure our sister, I knew perfectly well. Anywhere Boyo chose would be more than that.

And it is.

We have parked the bike and are strolling through Dockland, the seamiest part of Cardiff. The area of pimps and prostitutes, and violent crimes of passion, exciting stuff like that. The area in which no decent white girl is ever seen to set foot. Siriol will puke with fury when I tell her I've been here. We girls have spoken of venturing forth in this direction just for the hell of it. In the end she's proved to be just too faint-hearted. I hope for more reckless companions up at Oxford, ones with a taste for adventure.

'It's a club that we're going to,' Boyo guides me around a corner.

'I thought that we would be.' I giggle in anticipation and look over my shoulder apprehensively. 'Isn't this where policemen have to patrol in pairs?'

Boyo throws back his head and laughs, not bothering to reply. I'm hurt. 'No really. This is Tiger Bay, isn't it?' He grazes my chin with his knuckles.

'Stick by me, you'll be all right. It's time you emerged into the real world. The trouble with you, Boadicea, is that you believe everything you read. I'm going to have to complete your education this summer, otherwise you'll never survive up at university.'

I say nothing. I can't reply. I feel as though I've been struck. This is the closest that Boyo has come to criticism of me. How must I appear to him that he should have this impression of me? How little any member of my family actually knows about me. To them I am that uncomfortable creature to live with, an exceptionally clever child. As such, someone to be handled with kid gloves. I must take greater pains to reassure them, and make them less in awe of me. When I leave I should like us all to be much closer. Especially Boyo.

'I'm in your hands, Boyo.' I say it softly, meekly, though for one wild moment I'd thought to go complètely mad and confess that I'm not the little innocent that he imagines me to be. That I have had carnal knowledge of men from the age of ... well ... thirteen, if we're going for absolute honesty. But I decide against this unwise revelation, it can wait until another time. We arrive.

'This is it. This is the place.' Boyo steadies me. 'Don't let it go to your head, little one.' He smiles indulgently. I don't know what the hell he's talking about.

'No Name', is the sign above my head, twinkling in fluorescent pink neon. At the sight of its hot glow, so sinful and exotic in this shabby alley, my bowels churn impatiently. I'm already excited and even more so when we push our way through the double doors and enter the club. It is as glamorously seedy as I could have hoped for. Wait till I tell Siriol about this twenty-stone bouncer barring our way! Black as Blodwen's Bible, with teeth as white as my clothes, gleaming in a wide grin of welcome as he rècognises Boyo in the dimmed lights.

'Hiya, Boyo! Who dat den – de gurlfren?' And he goes off into peels of laughter, his great belly trembling over his trousers so that he has to hold it steady with both hands.

'How you doin', Wally?' Boyo slaps him on the shoulder and passes through. He doesn't introduce me, but simply signs the book 'and guest'. I don't know whether to feel piqued or not, I would have enjoyed seeing Boadicea Jones on those pages.

Inside we are in a different world. We've had to walk downstairs into a basement. Stairs which are garishly lit and covered with threadbare carpet so greasy that it would have been simpler to slide down them. There floats up the frenzied sound of people enjoying themselves, the regular beat of disco music on a juke box. A reggae number currently high on the charts. Siriol has every record by this group – her idea of sexy sounds. The smell that rises is hot and heady, a mixture of perfume and alcohol, and the animal scent that Boyo's leather clothing exudes. He is wearing his leather this evening, and he has hung several thin gold chains around his neck and sports a single gold earring in his left lobe. He looks absolutely magnificent. I pray that he won't go off with some woman and leave me a wallflower sitting in the corner.

'Don't go off and leave me now – will you . . .?' I am suddenly shy of being thrust amongst Boyo's friends. That unknown quantity, the ones that he so seldom brings to the house. I have been thankful for that in the past. I never thought that I'd be capable of concealing the jealousy that I'd feel towards any girl-friend of my gorgeous brother. I have never thought I'd be able to bear it if he'd come home with someone from London, kissing and canoodling in front of the rest of us, as Mavis likes to do with her latest. But fair play for Boyo, he's never put us through that embarrassing spectacle up to now. Am I to be subjected to it tonight? I couldn't bear to see Boyo in some awful girl's arms – not even just dancing!

He laughs, looking into my face, his eyes shifting onto my mouth. 'Hey,' he kisses me lightly on the upper lip, then on the lower. 'All ready?' Then he swishes the heavy curtain to one side and draws me into the 'No Name' club. It gives me the sensation of stepping straight into Hades. I have never felt so immediately at home anywhere before in my entire life.

Chapter 7

Zeus Bowen has been home a whole week and I still haven't seen him. All my excitement at the thought of his return has evaporated. I'm just angry he hasn't made greater efforts to get in touch. Oh, he's dropped in just in passing, had a cup of tea and a few casual words with poor old Blodwen – she's told me he asks after me – but apart from that, nothing.

It never has been easy, our getting together. But in the early days we made my studies the excuse, my interest in his work, the easy affinity between a scholar-poet and a pupil of outstanding ability. What could have been more natural than him spending time with me in my bedroom, my place of work, my book-lined and private world. The one where few were ever made welcome, not even Blodwen or other members of my family, just Siriol – and then Zeus Bowen.

Perhaps, and I make excuses for him, there is a particular reason for his caution. His wife has become suspicious, the witch Dilys has got the wind up. What I can't understand is that he has called in here at such odd hours, at times when he must have known that I would have been out shopping – he knows the routine of this house during the season as well as we who live in it.

'Did he say when he'd come again?' I'd asked Blodwen

asually. But she'd shaken her head vaguely, abstracted as usual. She really is getting worse and worse. I toy with the idea of asking her whether I should pop around to his house to say hello, thinking that it will sound ingenuous enough to be merely a friendly act instead of an intimate need. I must see him sometime before I leave this town – I can't just go, not like this. We'd made so many plans of how we'd meet in the future, all the nights and the weekends that we'd be able to spend together. He away from Dilys on the pretext of a poetry reading, a lecture, a television appearance. There was never any doubt in his mind, or anyone's come to that, that I'd be accepted by the university of my choice. I can't credit it now, but I was certainly adamant at one time about applying to Cardiff or Swansea, or Aberystwyth. Just to be that much closer to Zeus Bowen! The self-satisfied cunt!

Christ – why can't he at least phone me? Please!

We are short-staffed this morning, Boyo took the early train to London to attend the audition that his agent rang up about. It's for a television series on the line of 'Rock Follies'. meant for transmission around Christmas. Boyo says he won't get the part, and that irritated me.

'Why not you?' I said to him. 'Take a positive attitude for change, you may find it'll bring you luck.' And I hugged him, flinging my arms around his neck and kissing him noisily on both cheeks. He laughed.

'Wow! That'll bring me luck, kid. P'raps I should take you with me as a mascot.' Then he'd seen my eager expression and shaken his head. 'Not this trip, baby – but pretty soon, I promise. The minute I get some proper cash in hand, I'll take you up to the big city. You and I could raise quite a storm!'

Mavis had given a spiteful laugh, nudging Blodwen as she did so.

'I think we two are missing out on something here, older sister.' But Blodwen said nothing as usual. She probably hadn't even been listening.

'Funny without Boyo, isn't it—' I say now. And it does

seem strange with me doing the cooking. Frying the bacon, scrambling the eggs, crisping the triangles of sliced bread in the hot fat – all crusts removed for the touch of class that we pride ourselves on in this guest house. All that crap. Not that I'm not enjoying it, and not that I don't do it all very capably. It's making rather a nice change, knowing that Blodwen will be taking over my duties. Doing the rooms whilst I prepare lunch, her and Mavis. Because Mavis is hopeless when it comes to cooking, she just hasn't the feel for food, it's bypassed her altogether. If we let her loose in the kitchen we could forget about full board, they'd be begging to leave before the next meal. I said as much this morning when it became apparent that Blodwen wasn't capable of carrying on with the breakfast after she'd puked up in the sink.

'Atta girl,' I'd soothed, holding her haunches as she swooped over in a further retch. 'That's it, get it all up. She hasn't eaten anything yet – she must have a stomach bug.' I addressed the rest of the room, namely Mavis and Mrs Pugh.

'Yes, indeed, there's a lot of it about,' Mrs Pugh declared, pursing her lips.

Mavis merely groaned. She was suffering too, from the effects of a vile hangover. Since my trip to the 'No Name' club, I felt qualified to sympathise with her. Before then I had never been the victim of too much alcohol and so hadn't ever witnessed its after-effects without feeling sure that the sufferers were wildly exaggerating. If Mavis felt anything like I did the day after my night on the tiles, she might very well join Blodwen – at the sink.

'Who's to cook breakfast?'

'Not me.' Mavis managed to answer my question.

'Nor me, love. I do always burn things.' Mrs Pugh looked around proudly. She'd been making this claim ever since she'd been working with us, and had ruined an entire loaf of bread whilst making toast one morning in order to prove it. Scraping each piece to get rid of the charred surface with much satisfied cackling as she did so. And then expecting me

68

to serve it up in the dining room. Silly old fart.

'I'm so sorry, Boadicea love.' Blodwen had turned her green complexion in my direction. Her mouth was drained of all colour, merging into the rest of her face. She looked pitiful. Emotion tugged in my throat at the sight of her.

'Blodwen, you do look terrible, as ancient as I feel.' Mrs Pugh spoke as she slurped a cup of tea, spilling some of it messily down her cardigan. 'There now – look at me.' But none of us chose to, particularly not me. When you have been brought up as I have been, surrounded by beautiful faces, it jars to have to rest your eyes on countenances that fall so far short of standard. Mrs Pugh may have been worth her weight in gold to some, though I would question that the old bat was worth a ha'penny, but she would never be one of life's oil paintings. Unless the artist were one who chose his subjects for shock value, like Hogarth or Hieronymous Bosch. Hideous.

And so I'd taken over, the only one capable of control. And no complaints from the customers.

'Funny, isn't it,' I say it yet again, 'without Boyo?'

'Huh – you'd find it funny on your honeymoon, without Boyo!' Mavis's attempt at wit.

'There's only one female interested in honeymoons in this house, Hotpants,' I address a sizzling sausage with this retort, then wave it suggestively beneath my smouldering sister's nose. 'Lamentably lacking in edge or imagination, this exchange! It wouldn't have been if Boyo had been here, he has the exuberance to lift any conversation.'

'Now then,' Mrs Pugh butted in. Blodwen sinks down on a kitchen chair, clutching her stomach and trying to muffle a groan.

'Hey, Blod ...' Even Mavis looks concerned, though she's not the star of this show. 'Are you all right?'

'Of course she's not bloody all right. Go back to bed, Blodwen. We can manage without you.' I order her out of the kitchen with a flourish of my fork. And she does as I say, taking the hot water-bottle that I've filled for her. We've been filling hot water-bottles for each other for years –

nothing gives the same comfort when you're ill in bed. Mavis spurns them as being babyish, further proof of her insensitivity.

There are tears in Blodwen's eyes as I hand her the scalding rubber.

'Here, wrap this around it in case you burn yourself.' I pick up the woollen sweater which I discarded when I started cooking. I'm keeping a close watch on the contents of the frying pans, seeing that nothing overdoes. 'And go to sleep,' I say. 'Don't worry about a thing.'

'She's poorly. She's been looking bad for the past week – hey, Mavis, hold the tray steady. There's more bacon for that plate.' Blodwen has gone now and Mrs Pugh has seized the opportunity of presenting herself to the guests, on the pretext of clearing the cereal bowls and the finished grapefruit dishes. She enjoys getting in the dining room, given half a chance. Delighting in regaling us with how much older so-and-so is looking since last year, or how much the younger ones have grown. Mundane stuff.

'Well, well, well!' She bustles in now, bony elbows all over the place. 'Who'd have thought that Mrs Cadog Rhys could have aged so in just twelve months. Yes indeed! No exaggeration to say that I hardly recognised the poor creature – and as for that lovely boy, little Samson Evans! Well, he's huge, isn't he just! I made him stand up tall for me, he's right up to my shoulder. And no more than nine. Lovely boy!' She pauses only to put down her empties before snatching the large tray of fried food from Mavis. 'Oh, let me, there's a love, I'm just in the middle of hearing about poor old Llewellyn Hughes's haemorrhoids.'

'Very tasty with egg and bacon, Mrs Pugh,' Mavis comments. I think how bloody ravishing she looks with her hangover compared with how I looked with mine. Any sullen emotion on that face simply registers as sexy sensuality. To do with the darkness of lid and lash, and the shadow cast on the light eye. Her pout only succeeds in making the mouth more kissable. Mrs Pugh rounds on her, fit to take care of herself in any verbal display of fireworks. We are unpleasantly feline when Boyo's not around.

'I've had to place a nice soft pillow beneath his buttocks,' Mrs Pugh accused. '*Me*, the only one who thought to do it, only a small act of Christian kindness. Shame on you, young madam. And old Llewellyn Hughes been coming here for his holidays all these years too. He said now that it's the first moment of comfort he's enjoyed eating a meal on this visit.' And turning to include me too, she scolded, 'You young people should think of that, offering cushions.'

'To everyone, Mrs Pugh?' I ask innocently open-eyed. 'Or just those who suffer from what is it – haemorrhoids. And if so, how would we know?'

'How would we know?' Mavis giggles. Mrs Pugh has departed in a huff, refusing to be drawn by my childishness. It's the first time Mavis has giggled like this with me since – oh, I couldn't think when. Without the others around we could sometimes get on quite well, but it would be difficult to be as intimate with her as I could be with Boyo, or even Siriol. I think that her beauty creates its own barrier. Also Mavis has never been possessed of the same humour as me. She doesn't relish the blackness, doesn't transcend the tragic aspects of life by choosing to see the comic undercurrents. She'd be a dull fish indeed if she weren't so bloody decorative. But if she looked ordinary like the rest of us then she'd have to try harder in the entertainments department. The exceptions are the ones who have everything. Like Boyo.

I sigh now, thinking about him. Re-living the glories of our night out. But first I've answered Mavis's question about how to recognise haemorrhoids.

'If you bothered to read as many medical tomes as I do, Mavis, you wouldn't need to ask,' I say in a school-ma'amish way, but it doesn't daunt her at all.

'Why should any of us bother to find out about anything in this family when we've got a genius in our midst who can tell us at the drop of a hat.' I search for signs of rancour in her sultry expression but there are none.

'Blackcurrants,' I say.

'Beg pardon?'

'Blackcurrants, or in extreme cases,' I go on, 'entire bunches of grapes.'

'Not white grapes?' Mavis has caught on. Miracle of miracles!

'Precisely.' I expound. 'External piles, or haemorrhoids, resemble blackcurrants attached to one side of the anus – not to be confused with prolapse of the rectum. An uncomfortable state to be in where the lining of the rectum sticks out at the anus ...'

Mavis is holding a tea-towel to her mouth. Her eyebrows, which are all that I can see of her face, are bunched together in horror.

'Identification between the two conditions is relatively simple. Whilst piles, or haemorrhoids, are plum-coloured –'

'Or blackcurrant –'

'Right Mavis,' I smile approvingly, having been disappointed in the earlier display of squeamishness. 'In the other condition, the protruding tissue is pink –'

'Like – like candy floss!'

'Well,' I go slowly, best to keep her wilder fancies in check. Reality itself can create a more forceful image. 'More like the protruding finger-tips of a surgical glove, I would have said. Not quite so frothy.'

'Ah.' Mavis nods wisely. I can see that she has enjoyed this brisk barter of ideas. Perhaps I should assume some responsibility for her education now, teach her how to coax a conversation along so that it can lightheartedly take off. In the way that Boyo has undertaken my entry into the adult world, and the seamier side of life.

I sigh again now, the medical discussion being at an end. Not that I'm ever inclined to call a halt to any conversation of that gripping nature. That's one of the obsessions that I joyfully share with Zeus Bowen: a preoccupation with parts and functions. *A Dictionary of Symptoms* – erotica for the Welsh! That's how he'd described one of our favourite books. Riveting stuff. And full of poetic passages too, such as the description of *Allergic Rhinitis*, a complaint similar to hay fever. Or the causes for *Pain in the Face*, like *Tic Douloureux*,

Lockjaw, Bell's Palsy or the more modest *Gum Boil.* We have been much delighted by the particular line in philosophical fatalism doled out in these learned pages. Victims driven to the edge of insanity by *Tinnitus,* buzzing noises in the head, are told that they must learn to ignore what's described as a harmless, personal, background noise. That the treatment is either very simple, e.g. removal of wax, or almost impossible. If Joan of Arc had read *A Dictionary of Symptoms* and chosen to disregard the clamouring chorus between her ears as being harmless, personal, background noise she would never have been barbecued.

'You're sighing a lot this morning, Bo.'

'The frying fat has affected my sinuses – I'm trying to get more air aboard.'

'Truly?'

'Not truly.' I'm overtaken by an urge to tell Mavis all about the 'No Name' club. If he were here I'd be able to go all over it again with him. Siriol has gone away with her family to France, lucky thing. Unexpectedly, before I even had a chance to swank about my ride on the motorbike – let alone all the other things.

'No, not truly. I'm just thinking about Boyo not being here. I bet he doesn't come back tonight. I bet he doesn't come back all week.' I burst out in what sounds like petulant childishness. 'Just when my social life was getting off the ground. He promised to take me out with him again this evening.'

'He'll be back I expect, love.' Mavis slides her eyes over my face. I shake back my long fringe, which I have taken to wearing on one side. Like those politicians who go around pretending they are still small boys at prep school. People like Peter Shore, I'm thinking of. Peculiar only to the British, this particular type of man. Elsewhere in the world they are not so afraid to be seen to be adult. But then it was this country that produced Peter Pan.

'Here, let me.' Mavis draws back the offending strand and tucks it neatly behind my ear. 'It looks really great, your hair, this summer. You're going to be a wow amongst all those boys at Oxford. What is the ratio, twenty-five males to one

female?' There is wistfulness in her voice. I suppose to someone like Mavis who cares about these things, about good job-
prospects and getting on, money in the bank, it must seem
most enviable. Being in the position to pick and choose from
the best brains in Britain before anyone else has a chance
to nab them, before they are fully matured and let loose in
society. But I just laugh.

'I can't imagine what the bloody ratio is, I haven't gone
into it. I tell you what though, Mave,' I'm feeling reckless
now, but lower my voice. I don't want old Pughie to hear
this. 'I bet that nothing I do at Oxford, no place I get taken
to, will be anything compared to the "No Name" club!' And I
laugh again, hugging the memory to me, tantalising Mavis
into begging me to tell. Which, naturally, she does right
away. But I have to be careful. If I am going to spill the beans,
all of them, we ought to take the precaution of being in private.

'Look,' I say quickly before Mrs Pugh comes back, 'you
give me a hand here peeling the potatoes and things for lunch
after we've cleared this lot. Then I'll do the rooms with you.
Two of us together will get those beds done in no time. Give
me a chance to go into all the gory details,' I wink.

'Fancy that, then! Mrs Gwen Evans – five years younger
than me! Did you know that, you girls? *Younger!* And there
she is in there, sitting with the flesh hanging from her bones.
Cancer, I'd say. Elijah's sister went the same way, shocking
to see by the end. I haven't hinted as much to her, mind, but
if I looked like that I'd have myself seen to. Yes, indeed I
would.' Mrs Pugh compresses her lips, making a silent promise to herself. 'Oh, and another pot of tea for that young
couple in the window. Are they on honeymoon? They're not
talking. They've not said a single word to each other, not
the whole time they've been in there. But I went up to them,
and I asked if everything was to their liking, feeling the pot
to see if the tea was still warm. Cold as ice. Make them another
pot, there's a good girl, Mavis love. Nice to show a willing,
isn't it Boadicea, is that toast ready yet? There's people waiting. Phew!' She wipes her forehead with the back of her
wrist, relishing every second of service. But still prepared to

74

make out that she is being put upon.

'What is it, Mrs Pugh?' I say to her as if concerned. 'Are you sure that you're not doing too much running around now? At your age you should be taking it a bit easier. Let Mavis do all this, that's what she's here for. You stay back in the kitchen with me. Isn't that right, Mavis?' I look at Mavis slyly out of the corner of my eyes. But she is not interested in baiting Mrs Pugh, she is hardly concentrating on how many tea-bags she's putting in the young couple's teapot. I hope those honeymooners like their tea strong, I've lost count myself of the perforated envelopes she's dropped into the pot. She'll scald herself with boiling water next from the electric kettle. But I doubt if even that would register at this moment. Her mind is on me. For once her curiosity is focused on someone other than herself. I know what she's thinking too – how come this kid sister of mine's getting these thrills right under my nose, when I'm trundling along this summer like all the other summers just waiting for Mr Right to come along. Maybe kid sister can teach me a thing or two after all, and not just the junk she gets out of books either.

Mavis must wait and see just how much.

Chapter 8

'*But you didn't actually strip, Boadicea!*'

'I took my top off and showed my tits,' I answer happily. 'I was rather proud of them too. There are mirrored walls in the 'No Name', smokey glass, so that I could see plenty of images of myself. I would have been willing to do a complete strip, but it was late by then and people had plied me with so many drinks that I don't think I would have been capable to getting any more clothes off anyway. Not without help and that would have spoiled it. Boyo had to undress me for bed when we got home . . .'

'Boadicea!'

'Yes, Mavis?'

'Honestly!'

'What?'

I am really enjoying this, it is ten times the fun that I'd anticipated. Really fabulous. Mavis, I reflect, is turning out to be an even more appreciative audience than Siriol would have been. It makes me realise that I may have been missing out for years on the delights of sharing the outrageous secrets of one's dirty deeds. If I'm not careful I'll find myself revealing all to Mavis. Dreadful confessions of lascivious encounters over the years, when everyone thought that my head had been well into my textbooks, with no interest on the male physiology.

Mavis sprays herself lavishly with Barbie Roosevelt's perfume. The scent of it drifts all over the room, hard and spicy and intended for immediate seduction. But it doesn't work over in my corner. I am polishing the mirror, just coated with 'Sparkle' cleaner. I prefer the 'Sparkle' smell myself. It puts me in mind of swimming pools, and the vision of the bulging cocks of young boys, all shyly trying to conceal themselves. More sex in that than the squashed juice of ripe flora. As usual I am the one doing all the work. Mavis, whilst listening so avidly to my every word, is trying on Barbie Roosevelt's clothes. I fight down the alarmed feeling that the lady might make an unexpected entrance. If she came in now she'd have the fine sight of Mavis wearing her most expensive outfit. The one which even that slut keeps in a polythene cover. Pearly white satin sheath with a tiny crystal bolero – real cocktail wear for uptown Manhattan, if the television series are anything to judge by. Not my sort of thing, and not strictly Mavis's either. Too ordinary by far for her exotic looks. But Mavis looks sensational in it. When does she never? And she has now discovered that Barbie Roosevelt takes the same size in shoes as herself. Not like me. My feet are the size of boats. There is no chance in hell of me ever being able to get into these Cinderella slippers.

It looks as if we're going to be stuck with the Roosevelts all summer, her and the kids anyway. Elmer Roosevelt has to be back in Dallas by next week on business, but Barbie's mother has taken a turn for the worse. She collapsed three days ago and had to be rushed to the heart ward of Penmawr Hospital. Barbie looks tense and anxious all the time now, snapping irritably at her children, which sets up more friction than usual between them. Americans are hopeless at bringing up children. We've had families before staying with us and it's always the same – the parents are terrified of being seen to be in control. As if by exerting discipline they forfeit their children's friendship. What's so wonderful about having prattling brats as pals anyway?

Mavis pirouettes slowly in front of the wardrobe mirror. I have lost her attention. But not for long. She cups her voluptuous breasts in her hands in an attempt to flatten them. 'I haven't seen your tits for years,' she says to me, frowning at her own as if they don't please her at all. She's always complaining about the size of them, when almost any girl in the world would willingly swap them for the ones they've got. Except maybe Raquel Welch. Though perhaps she would these days. She's no spring chicken after all, there must be some sag in the profile, some tendency in those famous orbs to point at the pavement rather than towards heaven. A criticism which certainly couldn't be made of Mavis's superb pair. Or my own, such as they are.

'Oh, they're coming on.' I reply. 'Not in your league, Mavis. Mostly all nipple.' I put down my duster. 'Do you want to have a look?' And without waiting to hear whether she does or not, I take off my tee-shirt and stand before her in my tight jeans, tanned all over from the waist up. To my satisfaction I note the hardening of each nipple, due to the shock of the sudden exposure. Or perhaps standing half-naked in front of my blazingly beautiful sister is arousing me. It's possible.

'Sweet – really sweet, little dinky things!' Mavis moves over to touch them with her finger-tips. I suddenly get gooseflesh all over. 'Real little virgin's titties. Tilted.' She traces a line from my chin down my neck and around each small breast. No-one has ever touched them as gently as she's doing. It strikes me for the first time what a bloody marvellous time lesbians must have with each other. I didn't think so the other night when one of the lesbians at the 'No Name' had asked me to dance. I refused her rather mulishly. Now I see that I might have made a silly mistake. It's not usually in my nature to say no to new experiences. Maybe I didn't fancy that particular woman, she was too conventional for my tastes. She could have been any one of the wives here on holiday, wearing a navy blue shirtwaister dress over a hefty Spirella corset. And hair neatly permed and parted just off the crown. English, and well-spoken. Afterwards someone told me that she was a doctor with a practice in Bath. The 'No Name' club was a long way off her regular beat!

Now if one of the other girls had asked me that would have been a different matter. If that tall, dimpled actress with the husky voice and all the hair had, I'd have leapt at it. She was eyeing me from the moment I arrived with Boyo. But her girl-friend was with her, keeping a close guard, never straying from her side the whole bloody evening. Not even when the actress had gone to the lavatory. Really possessive. 'Isn't that Ursula what's-her-name, Boyo?' I'd asked him as soon as I'd seen her. She'd been on television only the evening before. 'That's her' he'd answered. 'But hers isn't the only famous face you're likely to see in here, kid. Just don't spend the whole evening asking me whether that's so-and-so. If you think it is then take it that you are right.' And he'd ruffled my hair into my eyes, laughing at me. 'My little star-gazer.'

Oh, but it was wonderful! I'd never before been among so many famous people. And knowing that I was, made me feel so much more important myself. As if I had earned the privilege of being there, as if I really was one of them. Established and successful. It made me see what a wonderful life I have ahead of me. And to think that no-one there had any idea that they were in the same room as their future Prime Minister! That made me laugh to myself.

I'm laughing to myself now, thinking about what Mavis has just said. How she'd described my breasts as being those of a virgin. Should I enlighten her, I wonder? Relish her amazement? 'Mavis,' I start to say, watching her face for the reaction. But she suddenly swoops forward and starts kissing my left nipple, and I stop talking. My cunt starts to throb, my clitoris is swelling.

More than anything in the world I want Mavis to fuck me.

It doesn't happen.

But it might have if we hadn't been disturbed. 'Telephone!' Mrs Pugh screeches up the stairs. Neither Mavis nor I utter a word. If she is as wet and excited as I am down below, then we're going to need a bath towel to mop up. As far as moving is concerned, forcing one foot in front of the other, it seems an impossibility. My entire body feels drained, paralysed but for that ravenous appetite simmering between my legs. I used to feel like this right at the beginning with Zeus, when I was still a virgin. He used to play with my nipples a lot then. But when we'd graduated to more basic stuff, the real in-and-out of it, there didn't seem to be so much time for the same foreplay.

'Telephone! Telephone you two up there – one of you better come and answer it!'

'Sod her!' I say savagely, pulling myself together. I look to see where my tee-shirt is, then I pull it over my head.

'Just as we were getting going,' Mavis whispers dreamily. She has the same expression as those girls in commercials extolling the virtues of one brand of soap powder over others. Getting sensual satisfaction out of extra-soft woollies, pressing their babies' boiled nappies up against their rouged cheeks and smiling rapturously straight into camera. She'd be terribly good at all that, Mavis. The perfect quality, guaranteed to promote sales of any product.

'Better answer it.' I leave hastily, curious as to why there is no embarrassment on Mavis's part. This isn't the first time she's played with another girl, it can't be. She's too self-assured, as if the whole incident is absolutely natural. I wonder which of her girl-friends it might have been. Knowing her awful friends, it would have been the idea of one of the men. There had been rumours of orgies taking place at weekends in the Vale, wife-swapping and suburban goings-on like that. Siriol told me that she'd been invited along by the bank clerk from Penarth. If she'd gone, she might have found herself being touched up by my sister. That image really intrigues me. As I run down the stairs I find that my spirits have soared. I am as high as a kite. Adrenalin pumping all over the place.

'Thank you, Mrs Pugh!' I sing out to that scowling harridan. 'Hello,' I burble into the phone, 'can I help you?'

The voice at the other end of the line sounds strained and subdued. I don't recognise it.

'Hello,' I say again. 'Boadicea Jones at your service.' Nothing

80

can bring me down, I am irrepressible. I'm thinking how thrilling it is to be on the verge of this whole new experience. Girls. Women. Other females. Why hadn't I thought of it before? It wasn't my imagination, there was a positive attraction blowing between me and that husky actress the other night. Some pretty strong current zooming across the club. If it hadn't have been for Boyo's West Indian friend monopolising me all evening something would have happened. If her girl-friend had allowed her a moment on her own. Never mind, there would be other times. And other actresses, no doubt just as alluring. And it wasn't as if I regretted dancing all evening with Boyo's pal, Darren. He was the best dancer there. A professional, the same as Boyo, but with no singing voice. It was Darren that encouraged me to do my semi-strip. When he had removed his shirt to a Latin-American rock number, I could see no reason not to do the same. And no-one restrained me, not even Boyo. I think he was proud of my lack of inhibition. He was behaving impeccably himself, seeing to it that I had a thoroughly good time on our first night out together. No flirting with other girls, nothing like that. Just lining up the drinks for Darren and me between dances, making sure that I knew he was at the bar waiting for me if things should get out of hand. Which they might have, after I'd removed my white jacket and starting really to let fly on the dance floor in my little boob-tube.

Several heavies had arrived after the pubs had closed, real tough guys. None of them were members, but they'd muscled their way past reception to get upstairs. And one of them had taken a fancy to me, tapping Darren on the shoulder as if in an excuse-me dance. But Boyo had sorted it out. He'd seen them off with the help of other regulars down there. 'You never need to worry with Boyo around,' Darren had whispered proudly to me. He was slender as steel himself, looking as if a puff of wind would blow him over. But I could feel the muscles in his arms as he held me and the strength of his torso as he whirled me around. Though there were enough of Boyo's supporters to demolish the tough boys who'd started pestering me, Darren lunged in with the rest of them. His blow would have been as unexpectedly vicious as a jack-in-the-box. An unknown force to be reckoned with.

'So – Boadicea Jones at your service, is it now?' The voice at the other end of the line sounds amused. I recognise this fresher tone immediately.

'Zeus!' I say. 'Zeus!' My second 'Zeus' is very different from the first.

Chapter 9

We are lying in our secret place far across the hollowed sand-dunes. It's overcast and might rain so there are few holiday-makers below us on the beach. If there were it would make very little difference to Zeus and me, no-one ever comes this far over. Not even courting couples or lovers like ourselves.

Except that we are lovers no longer.

I am naked, my clothes form a comfortable pillow beneath my head. My hands are clasped behind my neck, which draws my tiddly-wink titties even higher than normal. Squinting down at myself I see them as sprouting out just below my chin. Their peaks like two warts, puckered and pale. 'Tiddly-wink titties.' That's what Zeus has just called them, fondly but with infinite sadness. I am shocked by the change in him, still shocked though I have seen him twice since his return. But this is the first time that we have been together on our own. There is more to be shocked about than his appearance. He has put on weight, a lot of weight. Before he went to the States anyone would have justifiably described him as roly-poly; he is now absolutely *gross*! He must have gained at least two stones in the three months that he's been away. It is loose, flabby stuff as well, billowing around his middle like blanched swathes of bread-dough. As if it needs an expert chef to kneed it into shape, pop the whole lot into a hot oven and bring it out crisp and brown.

Lord knows there are enough such bodies sunning themselves each day around this bay, but out of respect or revulsion, I usually look the other way. Until they have made themselves rather more presentable, as the bronzing takes slow effect. Why brown fat should be more acceptable than white, I can't work out. Unless it is that it resembles less a barrel of lard. Lard, that offensively leukaemic substance.

He looks ill, my Zeus Bowen, terribly ill. As if he is on the brink of some sort of breakdown. I say some sort because I can't be sure of the cause. I wouldn't like to judge whether it is physical or mental. When I say mental I don't mean that he's actually gone soft in the head, gone 'do-lally' as our Northern guests say. But he's certainly under some emotional strain. One so intense that he's not even able to find his usual release in tears. When Zeus can't cry there really is something up!

'Tell me about it,' I'd said to him gently, whispering as he held me close to him. Was that only an hour since, just an hour ago? But he'd been unable to speak, incapable of speech. Until I was howling into the deserted dunes by the end. Begging. *'Please tell me ... please ... please ...'*

Still no reply.

That's when I decided to seduce him.

It hasn't worked.

Now as I lie here, hands no longer clasped behind my head, fingers idly plaiting the sparsity of my pubic hair, I wonder which one of us made this assignation. Was it me? Had I pushed for it? Had I whispered to him so ferociously that I simply *had* to see him or Christ only knew what I'd do, that the poor sod had granted me audience despite his own feelings – was that how this fiasco had come about? I look at my watch, I haven't got the whole afternoon to waste! I'm due back to make the evening meal, but I can't leave him in this state. Or leave myself, come to that. I am very upset too. This ... lump ... this mute animal object lying beside me has been the love of my life for five years, less a fortnight. And haven't I been his!

What has gone wrong? Is this how it is when 'love flies out of the window'? No communication, no point of contact at all, as if the two of us had never met.

I am so stunned by the situation, the strangeness of being with whom I've always considered to be my alter-ego without any intimacy between us, that I take the bruised feeling around my heart to be an indication of pain to come. If anyone should be crying it ought to be me, but at this stage of the game I still hold out hope. I am searching for a vulnerable chink, through which I can restore my lover to his former ardour.

'Were you faithful to me in America, Zeus?' It is the one question that I swore I would never ask him. All the time that he was away, I trusted that I'd be able to restrain myself. And it isn't as if I want to know now. God – I don't care how much homogenised American pussy he's screwed! What would it matter if he'd dipped his dick in every cunt from here to Dixie just so long as things were warm and strong between the two of us now! But all he's doing is staring dully ahead. Not answering, not reacting to this leading question of all questions. The one that we'd spent so many hours teasing each other about before he'd gone away. Perhaps he's too guilty to face me because of those frivolous American infidelities – perhaps that's the cause of his anguish. In which case I must reassure him that he has my forgiveness. He doesn't have to admit to them. There the matter is at an end. No confession needed.

'I don't mind if you weren't, Zeus.' I plait and re-plait my pubic hair like a child playing with the precious hair on its doll's head. The nervous movements draw his eyes. Would he enjoy seeing me masturbating, I wonder? Would that help? I widen my legs, not very much at the start, just enough to be able to slide my fingers between. I am parting the pubic hair, such as it is, so that my poor lover can see how I am manipulating my clitoris. It is already swollen from our very recent encounter, when I attempted to coax Zeus's limp penis to life. He had been unwilling to let me take down his trousers so I had been reduced to lifting the flaccid object, as best I could, through the flies that I had to undo.

When I think of all the times that we'd feared for the fastening on these very same pants! His cock waving enthusiastically at the first sight of me, when I still hadn't removed one garment. 'If those seams go, Zeus Bowen,' I used to warn him, 'I'm not sewing them together again, you needn't think I bloody am!' 'Ooh, but you'd surely do a small favour like that for a man, wouldn't you, Boadicea? When I have taught you to do so much else ...'

And for that smooth-tongued bugger, I'd come on our dates with a needle and thread tucked into my pocket! Never intending to put them to any use, but just as a running joke between us. It stands to reason that Dilys, his wife, would recognise another woman's stitch in her husband's breeches. It's on small details such as these that adulterers falter.

Though my clitoris is engorged with blood, I am still dry. This sea air is drying, visitors always complain of its effect on their complexions, and I am as exposed now as it's possible to be. Each leg is lying at the furthest angle away from the other, I must seem excessively athletic to poor Zeus who will even have trouble clumsily struggling to his feet when we leave this hollow. But I'm not thinking about going home at this moment. I don't want to go home, ever, not if it means never coming here with Zeus Bowen again. Tears gather somewhere in the middle of my brain. It is only a matter of time before they seep out through my eyes. How unfair that lubricating liquid seems in such ready supply up top, when there's such a fucking dearth of it down below.

To make matters worse I now have sand in my snatch. Bloody great ... just what every seductress needs! I remove my fingers to my mouth, being careful not to give myself a fish-flavoured sand-sandwich, but spitting out saliva onto my finger-tips. Then I start all over again in my slit.

It is uncomfortable. But I am unwilling to break the spell, for I have got Zeus Bowen's full attention now. And I'm too frightened to look in case I'll be disappointed, but I can't imagine, knowing this man as well as I do, that he isn't getting excited too. I make a decision.

'I'm standing up, Zeus. But don't you move.' I rise gracefully to my knees and then to my feet, as if dancing, just like a ballerina in one unbroken movement. He'll appreciate that. I purposely twist as I do so, giving him a half-view of my raised buttocks. My arse-hole has driven him completely insane in its day.

Oh, Zeus ... Zeus ... my lovely lover ... desire me again ...

A terrible wave of despair is beginning to engulf me. Though I am standing caressing myself, above that one person whom I most want at this moment, I think he's falling asleep ...

The thought comes to me that he's on something, some drug, special dope that he has become keen on in the States. It could explain everything. His pallor, his emotional indifference to me, his lack of energy. Above all it could explain this impotence, an impotence so out of character with the man I have known and loved for so long. But who can I ask? Do I go to his wife and say, 'Pardon me, old girl, but how do you find your husband since his return from the United States of America? Pretty futile fuck now, wouldn't you agree?' How would Dilys know anyway? These two haven't screwed since she came out of the Ark, and ravaged the boy Zeus!

But I can ask old Blodwen if she finds him strange. She's seen him enough times when he's called in. She's been a good friend to Zeus over the years, remembering those times when my father was alive and such an encouragement to Zeus's writing. If old Blodwen only knew it she's been invaluable to our affair. How often he'd drop in ostensibly to pass the time of day with Blodwen, to have a cup of tea and a cake. And then steal along to my room, when all the time she thought that he'd left the house altogether. That's the advantage of living in a big old house such as ours. There are plenty of exits for easy unobtrusive escape.

But my mind has wandered back to happier times. I put my clothes back on my body, which is starting to shiver now.

And I lay down on the chilling sand and huddle for warmth against the dead—alive lump who is lying there.

He is asleep.

I kiss his unconscious lips very gently and practise mind over matter. However hard I strive I can't convince myself that these snortling bursts of rancid breath blowing in my face are really the stuff of romance. But I am in love with this repulsive wart-hog. Whether he wants me or not.

After about an hour has passed I wake up. I look at my watch in a panic, but it's all right – I've got half an hour to get home and start the meal. Mavis will have guessed I'd be a little late and will have got things in motion. I intimated, without saying who I was meeting, that I had a romantic assignation this afternoon. Mavis adores intrigues. She won't rest until she finds out who it is. She'll never know.

I look around. Zeus Bowen must have gone for a pee. He is nowhere in sight, and his coat has gone. The corduroy jacket, pockets bulging with notebooks, pencils, cigarettes, always a canned beer and several slabs of chocolate, that I am so fond of. I'm alarmed. Tears gather and start to fall down my cheeks. Can he have gone off alone like this? Zeus, of all men? I dig my hands into the pockets of my old rain-coat, the shabby one I wear when I don't want anyone to look at me. I'm searching for a hanky, something that I can comfortably cry into. That's what I'm doing now. Sobbing uncontrollably, louder and louder, screaming in competition with the gulls.

Chapter 10

'There's a postcard from Blodwen here!' Mrs Pugh is excited, she's read it already, but is pretending she hasn't. 'Oh, what does that lovely girl say?' Mavis takes it from her, my hands are full of chicken breasts and legs. Their colour reminds me of Zeus Bowen's belly, those weeks ago on the sand-dunes. At the memory something constricts in my throat.

It's pathetic how I miss Zeus Bowen in my life. If it were not for the other things that are going on I might seriously have thought of killing myself. Perhaps not *seriously*. Murder has been more constant in my mind than suicide. Being the positive course of action. I have discussed it with Siriol, my friend, who is helping us out whilst Blodwen is away on her convalescent trip.

'Siriol, tell me, have you ever contemplated murdering anyone?' She was shocked to be asked.

'You've got to be joking!'

'No, seriously. When any of your chaps let you down, you know. Did you feel furious enough to do them in?' We were walking back with the shopping, purposely dawdling, because Siriol was hoping to catch a glimpse of the drummer of the group who are on at 'Shingles'. She'd been told that he was staying in our street at the Garth Guest House. If we had room in our place she'd have willingly paid for his bed and board, but we're packed out like sardines this fortnight.

Just the time for Blodwen to decide to go away! She'd been advised to do so by Dr Parry, otherwise, he said, she wouldn't be able to see the summer season through. No-one seems to know what exactly is wrong with Blodwen, and if they do know then some fucker has decided not to let me in on the secret. But I was glad to see her go. To tell the truth it is much nicer without her here. Though I'm unable to put my finger on why, she makes me feel guilty about leaving her. About going off to university in September. I think she must guess that I regard this as the end of home for me, that it will never be the same again. That I shall rarely if ever come back to this place.

And certainly not now that Zeus and I are all washed up. When I think hard enough about that, I stop feeling so sorry for myself. That's when the murderous rage starts to boil.

'Chop off their balls, you mean, Bo?' Siriol is very succinct when she wants to be. It's one of the reasons that I have her as my best friend.

'That sort of thing,' I answered with care. I must consult my medical library as to whether forceful removal of bollocks can actually cause the victim to die. I'm not certain if excruciating pain is sufficient to assuage my sense of personal grievance. Or whether the victim should be required to pay with his life. I'd have to think about that one.

'Many times,' Siriol said thoughtfully. 'But don't you get into the most terrible trouble for violence of that kind? In my view, you see, the end result wouldn't really have justified the act. Why go to jail for some daft twerp who didn't manage to see your true worth?'

Siriol has spent a highly rewarding holiday in Brittany. The wine, which she claimed they drank at every meal of the day, including breakfast if I read her right, released her libido no end. She has become a dedicated Francophile. This drummer that she's after, the one playing at 'Shingles', is French. That's why, to quote her, 'I 'ave ze 'ots for 'im!'

But having her to confide in is such a release for me I can

forgive any nationalistic clap-trap. At least she's not fallen for the National Front.

'How does it feel this morning – your broken heart?' She asked then. She believes, because I have led her to believe, that I had an unhappy romance in her absence. Whilst she was in Brittany with her parents. I've told her about my visit to the 'No Name' club with Boyo, and she automatically assumes that I met this person there. The one who's now left me in the lurch. But one thing she's relieved about is that I'm no longer a virgin.

'Now you and I can really go on the town!' She whooped when I'd broken the news. And perhaps that is what I need to take my mind off the whole thing. It isn't as if Zeus Bowen is around so that I might bump into him. He's up at the Edinburgh Festival and will be for another ten days. I have checked. I haven't been able to tell Siriol about Zeus Bowen. She would feel betrayed over me having kept the secret for so long, I know that. And I need her too much as a friendly shoulder to lean on to take the risk of fouling it up. Though Mavis and I have become closer than we have ever been before, like real sisters, no longer rivals, that's not the same sort of friendship. Too much family is involved. Siriol is a pal, I don't care what opinion she has of me. And the other way around. And we're the same age too, that makes a big difference.

'Read the postcard out, Mavis.' I command from behind my poultry pieces. Boyo will be back to see to these in no time at all. He's gone to see to the loose cap on his front tooth, to have it cemented in more securely. Siriol has begged a lift on the back of his motorbike, crafty bitch. Just a chance to get her arms around him. I know.

'Having a wonderful time – a real rest. Food no patch on home. Missing you all. Feel guilty to think of everyone working but me. Love and kisses, Blodwen.'

'Is that all?' I ask, suddenly cross.

'Ah, bless her,' Mrs Pugh says sentimentally, wiping the corner of each eye with her pinafore ostentatiously, to show that she cares for our older sister more than we do.

'That's all.' Mavis turns the card over and studies the picture on the other side. 'Looks pretty,' she says without any real conviction.

'What is it a picture of?' Mrs Pugh sits expectantly with a cup of tea in her hand, a child who expects to be told a fairy story by the teacher. I dump the poultry pieces on the table and seize the card from Mavis.

'It has sky in it and some water.' I peer at it triumphantly. 'Oh yes, and some flowers in the foreground. Satisfied?' It is horrible of me, I know. I want to stop talking to Mrs Pugh in this vile way, but I can't. If we had a cat in the house I would be able to kick that, just to give vent to my feelings. But she's thick-skinned, she doesn't notice, I tell myself. That's when I've been particularly nasty. Today is not one of those days. In fact the opposite. Boyo is back and has brought with him a friend who is to help out as well as Siriol. Mrs Pugh is to be given a paid holiday. It was she who pointed out that she had not had a summer holiday for years. Not me, though I'd been machinating in my mind for long enough, God only knows. But her serving stint in the dining room paid off and handsomely. One of those old duffers has invited her back to his place, to travel with him. It's the widower, Llewellyn, I think. The sufferer of haemmorhoids.

'Between you and me,' I confided to Mavis when we heard of her invitation, 'I believe that she's been up in his bedroom helping to see to them, easing his pain. Popping the pessaries in place!'

But Mavis, so incurably romantic, has a feeling that we may not see Mrs Pugh again. She thinks that it all may end in matrimony. My foot! Siriol also thinks that this may be the case. I have managed to work old Siriol into the same loathing of Mrs Pugh as me. But when I hear Siriol speak as sharply to the silly bat as I do, I do feel a twinge of pity. After all you shouldn't victimise people. So perhaps I shall start crossing fingers that this geriatric marriage takes place between them after all. That way we will be rid of putrid Mrs Pugh once and for all. I'm forgetting that by going away from here, I shall be ridding myself of her anyway. But then what will become of Blodwen? How will she manage to run this place without either of us through the next winter? What will happen at the height of next summer's season? Has anyone else bothered to worry about that apart from one? Will no-one bring up the subject?

Boyo and Siriol have returned, I can hear the sounds of the back-firing machine. As can most of the street. This morning the French drummer that Siriol is so keen on stopped outside our house to admire the motorbike. But by the time I'd called Siriol who was up the top cleaning the bathroom, alas, her idol had moved on. Perhaps she hopes to interest him by being seen riding pillion. If I know Siriol she's hoping to kill two birds with the one stone – nab my gorgeous brother and catch the frog.

I wonder what Boyo's friend will be like? He's had to stop off in Cardiff first, seeing some distant relative. 'Half Welsh is he then?' I ask Boyo casually. However many strangers pass through these portals I experience a certain frisson when it is somebody brought in by one of the family. 'No, not half-Welsh, Boadicea,' he replies mockingly. And further than that he doesn't say, I wonder who his friend will be suitable for? Mavis, Siriol or me? Now that Mrs Pugh, oh ... and Blodwen will be out of the running.

Boyo and Siriol burst into the kitchen laughing, exuding that special gust of fresh air that comes with riding on the bike. Siriol is shaking out her long sandy hair and wrinkling her little freckled nose. She has grey eyes the colour of one of the pebbles on Pebble Beach, but in certain lights they turn green. They are looking as green as pale bottle glass now. Does Boyo find her attractive? I can ask this question without minding if the answer might be 'yes'. Boyo is too beautiful to keep him all to myself, and I find talking about him behind his back to Siriol highly satisfactory. According to her, the incidence of incest, particularly in the Celtic countries, is far higher than statistics would have one believe. And that contrary to popular belief intercourse between siblings does not necessarily result in a sub-standard foetus.

'I'm flabbergasted!' I said to her when she announced that.

'Why flabbergasted, Bo? You're the one who knows all these things, these riveting morsels of information. I read it somewhere, the article claimed that civilised nations were only taught the taboo of incest so that the fabric of society as we know it should not be impaired ...'

'I know all that bilge, Siriol,' I interrupted her with some impatience. 'And you didn't read it anywhere. It was me who told you when we knew for sure that we were doing *Hamlet* for 'A' Level, the day Esmée Morgan, in the third form, left school to have her brother's baby – you remember?'

'That's it, I remember now. Well, it's no surprise, you are the one who knows everything. But,' Siriol had screwed her eyes up in perplexity, 'then what are you flabbergasted over?'

'I'm flabbergasted, Siriol, by you quoting these facts to me the minute after we've stopped eulogising about Boyo's body.'

'Well he is your brother, Boadicea.'

'So?'

Siriol had snickered suggestively, then raised her eyes to the ceiling, humming the while.

'You filthy bitch, Siriol Williams!' I stared at her, shocked. It's one thing to have admitted the loss of my virginity, but no reason to reveal the full depth of my depravity to Siriol. Not yet.

'As if I'd ever dreamt of Boyo in that way. Nice girls don't entertain carnal thoughts about their brothers.'

'I bet!'

'Honestly, Siriol, you're incorrigible.'

'Sure. Sure I am. Tell you for nothing – if I had a brother looking like Boyo I'd have got into his bed years ago. That's the difference between us, Bo. Mind you, he's looking better now than he ever has. It's the beard mostly, but he's dressing differently as well. More macho, isn't it?'

'Macho!' My lip curled scornfully. 'You read too many women's magazines. "Macho" – straight out of *Cosmopolitan*!'

'Never mind that, let's get down to the basics. Would you fuck him if given the opportunity?'

'What do you think, Siriol?' We'd looked at each other. This friendship gets better every day.

This morning I have decided to tell Siriol about Mavis and me in the Roosevelts' bedroom. We are in the same room now, clearing up after Barbie Roosevelt and her children. It's not being disloyal towards my sister, it's just that I do so enjoy all this sexual talk with Siriol. And I'm feeling, we both are, just a little bit over-excited at the thought of Boyo's pal arriving this afternoon. Boyo has promised us all a trip over to the club tonight. Mavis is coming with us, which disconcerts Siriol.

'It's not that I don't like Mavis, Bo,' she is wailing.

'Doesn't matter to me if you like her or not, Siriol. I didn't like her myself until a couple of weeks ago. But when you get to know her a bit better ...!'

'Oh, I should *hate* to get to know her any better!' Siriol cries out in alarm. 'Just looking at her is too much. I'm finding it humiliating working alongside her. I find myself staring at her all the time. She's so gorgeous, it's hypnotic. I can't tear my eyes away.'

'What do you think it's been like for me all these years?' I say so gloomily that Siriol starts laughing. 'Bloody marvellous!' I deliver the lines as a tragedienne. 'We're introduced to people, the two of us, and the eyes flicker over me as if I'm not there at all. Human animals are fatally drawn to beauty. Like butterflies and flowers. I've had it all my life, with the three of them, Mavis, Boyo and Blodwen.'

'Yes, I admit Blodwen is very good-looking. Different, not so exotic ...'

'Well,' I spring to Blodwen's defence, which surprises me. 'She's gone off a bit recently, but on a good day her facial structure is actually better than Mavis's.'

'Huh, I'd like to see that!' Siriol sighs enviously. Then she burst out, 'Hell – does she have to come with us tonight? You said she has her own set, that she never goes anywhere with Boyo anyway.'

I don't answer for a moment, I'm thinking about it. About Mavis and the way she's been seeing less and less of her ghastly crowd. She's beginning to show a spot of good taste in her old age. Some of my sense is starting to rub off on her.

She seems to be a little wistful that Siriol and I spend so much of our time together, huddling in corners, whispering and giggling. Siriol and I are doing the bulk of the work, which could leave her much more time to scoot off with her lot. But she hangs around the house more than she used to, showing an interest in joining in our conversations. She'd be interested in this one, since it's all about her favourite subject.

'I don't think that I'm going to be able to relax if Mavis is with us. I know that we won't have such a good time. Everyone will be wanting to get off with her. Well they will, won't they? What sort of a look-in will we get?' Siriol grimaces at the mirror, rolled the pupils of her eyes so that only the whites are visible. With her fingers she pulls down the corners of her mouth, revealing a long expanse of slippery raw gum. She looks like one of the inmates of the Cawr Idris lunatic asylum. You can see them strolling through the grounds. Taking the air with as much dignity as they can muster, like retired colonels on the esplanade at Eastbourne. Something out of Somerset Maugham. Except that the frenzied progress of these poor sods is out of kilter, limbs flung in all directions. Jaws slavering in alarmingly genial grins of welcome. But still we all wave back, thinking no doubt there but for the grace of God go I.

Merely a clichéd turn of phrase. The belief in a deity has nothing to do with it. But I am profoundly interested in the various forms that insanity can take. Very many of the mad are not enclosed in our asylums. My thoughts dart to Zeus Bowen. It is with great effort that I wrench them away.

'If the wind changes you'll stay like that, Siriol, so stop it this minute!' I am imitating Mrs Pugh's shrill way of talking, the knack she has of making every pronouncement sound like a scolding. She has softened since old Llewellyn 'Haemmoroid' Hughes's invitation, I must say. She's almost girlish. Simpering. We let her off early this morning to prepare for her visit. 'I've washed everything down to my Sunday-best corsets, they were only new from the Co-op at Easter and I can't have had them near me more than the twice.'

'What have you been wearing to chapel then, Mrs Pugh?'

I asked her with every intimation of interest. Siriol nudging, egging me on from behind. The reply came juicy with that special excitement that women inject into exchanges of an intimate nature.

'To tell the honest truth of the matter, I've been wearing my old Sunday-best ones. There's still life in them, see. And now isn't that just as well too!' She smirked in a special way, in the direction of Mavis, as if the two of them shared the privilege of being women of the world whilst I was still merely a child. But I persisted. Siriol's elbow was pressing the small of my back.

'How's that, Mrs Pugh?' I gazed with innocent eyes.

'Now then, young Madam, never you mind – asking such questions indeed! Whatever next!' She'd have had a coronary if she knew the experienced cock-sucker I am. And how much I thrive on cunnilingus.

Siriol slowly rearranges her features. 'If the wind had changed and I'd stayed like that it might have been an improvement.' She sounds doleful. I remember what it is that I am going to tell her about Mavis. It's my job to cheer her up, show her how to re-assess the situation and that trying to compete with Mavis's spellbinding appearance may be going about it the wrong way. Competition is altogether unnecessary if I'm reading the situation right. Christ knows, I've thought about it often enough since it happened.

'I'm not so sure that Mavis will be going after any of the male talent that you'll be interested in, Siriol.' I am giving a meaningful pause. But she doesn't even glance in my direction. She is examining her profile, scrutinising the outline of her sharp chin. She's put on a bit of weight in France, old Siriol, but it looks nice enough. Most of it has gone onto her buttocks, making them eminently smackable. They stick out like two spongy pin-cushions. Boyo has already pronounced his approval. He claims to be a bum person, as I already knew. He plays around, tapping mine often enough.

'D'you think that all this fat I've put on has given me a double chin, Bo? Be honest, I don't mind.'

'You're not listening,' I say.

'I am. You've just said that Mavis and I won't be going for the same blokes. But that's not the point. I'd like to see anyone choosing me over her, whether she wants them or not. I'm always going to end up being second choice, that's what I don't like the idea of, Bo. Except,' she brightens, 'there is Boyo. She won't be going for him, will she? But then,' her face clouds over again, 'I expect you've probably got ideas in that direction.'

'Siriol, don't be so daft!' I slap her lightly around the head. 'And *listen*. The other day,' I lower my voice dramatically to give my piece of gossip the greatest effect, 'Mavis made a pass at me.' I stand back to await the reaction.

Siriol twists from the mirror where she is studying her breasts, dragging her loose shirt tightly over the contour. Like me she doesn't wear a bra, but she doesn't get away with it quite as successfully. Her chest has the same solid quality as her buttocks, highly muscled and somehow all of one piece. Whereas I am skinnier, I appear more fragile and more feminine. My curves are definitely curves, whilst Siriol's are – slopes. But her next words confound me.

'I don't blame her.' She says quite matter-of-factly. 'It's your legs. They turn everyone on.'

Chapter 11

We are all at the 'No Name'. Mavis is dominating the floor with Darren, the guy that I spent so much time dancing with the last time I was here. He hasn't got eyes for anyone except Mavis this evening, but I don't mind about that. Not one bit. Joyo's guest, Saul Polanski, has arrived and both Siriol and I are still suffering from the after-effects of the introduction. I am in love.

I lust passionately after this person with every pore, all the nerve-endings from the top of my body to the bottom, not to mention my screaming sexual organs (my cunt has been drenched since I set eyes on him!), but it isn't just lust. I know that.

'I'm in love with him – it's love at first sight, Siriol.' I don't know how I am able to say it so calmly, not when my bowels have turned to water. I fart, but since we are in the particularly gamey confines of the ladies lavatory I don't bother with an apology. Instead I spray a deluge of Siriol's French perfume over my shoulders. She got it duty free coming back on the boat, so I feel the extravagance is in order.

'This is the way I can tell,' I continue, talking loudly over the sounds of Siriol's piddle tinkling away in one of the lavs. 'If he had some kind of an accident which left him paralysed from the neck downwards, I would still agree to become his wife. Without martyring myself, I mean. I think that's the true test of love. Or do I mean that's the test of true love?' Saul Polanski, my idol, my aim for tonight (and for the rest of my living days) has introduced me to a delicious drink called a Harvey Wallbanger. I am just a little bit intoxicated.

'Well,' Siriol's voice is muffled. By the further plopping sounds from behind the door, she has obviously decided to go on to bigger things in there.

'Siriol,' I say, 'that's hardly sophisticated.' We are in a night club after all.

'He'd still have his mouth.' She shouts above the swishing of tissue paper. We are mercifully alone in this stinking hole without the inhibiting presence of fellow guests.

'Not the same though is it, Siriol?' I have to keep reminding myself that Siriol still considers me an inexperienced innocent compared to herself.

'Depends on the tongue, the length and the strength of it.' Her voice rises higher to compete with the cistern. I slurp more perfume in combat, choosing now to breathe through my mouth. As when dealing with Cindy Roosevelt's nappy offerings.

'I've got diarrhoea. I shouldn't think anyone would have much to complain of about Saul Polanski's tongue, Bo!' Siriol emerges. 'Best wash my hands, no hot water I bet. No bloody towel either and this fucking hot-air machine won't work - what a dump this place is!'

'Divine, eh, Siriol? The life of depravity suits me down to the ground. I'm thinking of foregoing my studies and becoming a hostess somewhere like this. I'm considering London. What d'you say? Why don't the two of us give it a try?' I favour her with one of my brilliant smiles, that I've been flashing at Saul Polanski for the past hour or so. Though it seems to me that he and I have been intimates all our lives. Siriol pulls up her skirts to adjust her minute pants, barely more than a stripper's G-string. We are both wearing them, hers are emerald green and mine are shocking pink, from a small shop that we've discovered in Barry Dock that specialises in such marvellously tawdry items. I should have shown Mrs Pugh the 'peek-a-boo' bra that I bought at the same time. Scarlet satin with holes for the nipples to poke through. Why hadn't I thought of wearing that tonight! I could have casually flipped my shirt open to allow Saul Polanski a peep, à propos of nothing at all – just to steer the mood of the moment along the right lines ...

'You're going to find it heavy weather fitting it all in.' Siriol is intent on bringing me down to earth. 'What with wiping the intellectual slate clean; depriving the nation of its next female Prime Minister; playing Florence Nightingale, wife and sexual acrobat to a paraplegic; and hostess, and doubtless honest whore, to the clientele in some seedy London night club –'

'I've got plenty of energy. I'm young.' I blaze away at my fly-blown reflection in the mirror. Radiant.

'You'd be dead before twenty-five. Besides, it would be a dreadful waste of a brain.' Siriol's aching regard for my distinguished academic achievements goes beyond mere envy. She, herself, will barely scrape enough 'A' levels to get into a teacher training college from which she will emerge merely qualified (if she manages to complete the course) to teach in the most elementary of schools. 'Infants are just about all I can aspire to!' She says in moments of wry self-mockery. She is more of an intellectual snob than me, but I hold her in no less affection because she hasn't the knack of passing meaningless school examinations. I think she'd make a first-rate night club hostess, with me.

I stare at myself from top to toe. 'Christ! I'm not looking bad tonight, Siriol!' And I'm not. I am wearing a black shirt of Boyo's, just that, tightly belted with a wide black patent belt that Mavis generously offered to lend me. Mind you, she has borrowed the lace wedding dress that I bought for fifty pence from the Baptist Noddfa jumble sale. I've had it, more correctly I've treasured that dress ever since I was twelve and only worn it for dressing-up sessions in the house. I didn't ever intend it for dancing. But looking at Mavis in it tonight I see that one shouldn't keep such things in sanctified safety. If it gets torn·to shreds (and I see that the hemline is already suspiciously uneven!), well, it did only cost me fifty pence. What's that as a price for having a good time! And I needed this belt to look as I do now. Without it, Boyo's shirt would be half-way to my knees instead of just covering my G-string. 'Like a mini-dress! Filthy!' Mavis had purred her approval. 'Did they really wear them that short?' Siriol and I are just too young to remember the minis. But I have studied the fashions of the sixties and I know how high hemlines reached. Talk about reaching, I shall have to be careful whilst dancing. These little panties don't have any back covering, simply a string which goes in between the buttocks. Only our pubic hair is actually hidden. From the back it seems that I have nothing on at all beneath Boyo's shirt. I thought all this out before leaving home, but I'm not sure that anyone else has yet got the point. I have managed to let Saul Polanski know that I am wearing a scrap of shocking pink, however brief, between my legs. In hoisting myself onto the high bar stool at his side I deliberately lifted a long, lean thigh so high that he'd have to be blind not to have caught that tantalising glimpse of my crotch. And I did it so gawkily, so much in the manner of a coltish child, that I doubt whether he began to guess that I knew what I was doing.

Or do I underestimate Mr Polanski?

Of one thing I'm quite certain – he has not fallen for Mavis.

'Well, Bo, the legs are on display – if that's what you mean. And you can never fail when that is the case.' Poor Siriol, her lack of leg-length is another sore point. Comparing us, I try not to notice that her waist is about level with my crotch, but the reason for that is that this evening I am wearing my only pair of high-heeled sandals. They are ridiculous, strappy things, which I bought early in the season. Not long after Mavis had arrived back from Bristol with her usual collection of devastatingly daft (and divinely desirable) footwear. But when I tentatively tried them on this evening, both Siriol and Mavis shouted ouc their approval. I'm finding it fun getting dressed up with the girls.

Now on impulse I twist around, tilt my bum in the air and

bend over to touch my toes. Just like a pin-up out of *Men Only*, naked from the higher point of the division of buttocks, right down to my race-horse ankles on their spindly heels. I grin at Siriol's admiring face in the mirror.

'What d'you think, kid?'

'I think – absolutely sensational, darling ...'

My eyes suddenly meet the mocking dimples of Ursula, the actress, the enchantress that I'd been hoping would be here this evening. Until I'd met Saul Polanski, that is. She is emerging from one of the furthest closets, the sound of the cistern gurgling behind her. She must have been in here all along and heard every word. Siriol is staring at her, she recognises the face. There have been posters all over the place this past week, advertising her play which is soon starting its pre-London tour at the Royal Theatre in Cardiff. It would be a difficult face to overlook. That's not counting the lion's mane of hair. Siriol is swallowing nervously.

'Oh ... hello,' I say feebly, still in position. It seems so anti-climactic to just straighten up. Perhaps we can remain like this the entire evening, the three of us. Ursula elegantly leaning against the lavatory door. Siriol just standing, struck-dumb and slack-jawed. And me with my tight arse bared to the four winds, my face at my feet, conversing on some interesting topic. How about the irony of rhetoric for starters?

The matter is taken straight out of my hands. Ursula prowls in my direction. Before I have had time to clear my throat of the congestion that is gathering there – due, no doubt, to my upside-down position and the tension of the times, I feel her tapered talons tampering with my G-string. She is lifting my shirt higher, right up to my waist now, and running her hands over the separate globes of my buttocks.

And more ...

I am caught, I'm completely helpless. I remain, like a marionette pinned in position. Any strain that I felt in the muscles of my limbs just seconds ago has vanished. The only sensations that I'm conscious of are in my cunt. My little G-string is dangling down around my knees, my eyes are fixed upon that neat juncture where the strings attach themselves to the shiny pink satin. But I still see the dark stain along this lush gusset, the damp that has accumulated from the excitement of this extraordinary evening. I have completely forgotten Saul Polanski – ah, what treacherous infidelity! I am wracked and trembling with desire nevertheless and if he were to enter this place, here with Siriol crouched on the floor in her astonishment, I would surrender my body to him without a struggle.

Except that for now Ursula has it.

I'm groaning, saliva is pouring around my gums. And I'm starting to rotate my hips around some hard and insistent pressure inside me. Up and down, it's going, up and down, up and down ... My eyes are tightly shut, I don't want to have to see anything at all. If I take another look at Siriol's idiotic pose, I shall burst into hysterical screams of laughter. And I don't want to do that. I want this to go on and on. Even though I know that quite soon it will be all over. Because now the two movements, mine and the glorious spreading pressure inside me, are working together and going much faster ...

I plunge both my hands down and hold whatever it is rigid against my exploding clitoris. Pressing as hard as I've ever pressed anything. And I'm moaning, I'm almost weeping, I am terribly upset. I am in an emotional turmoil. As if I shall burst all over this place, over Siriol, who is now engaged in frantic activity of her own between her legs. But as I focus my dazed eyes upon her jerky motions they cease, and she falls back against my ankles. Then turns her face upwards. Her expression is one of total exhilaration. Ursula kisses us both. First Siriol and then me.

Bending down to reach Siriol means that she has to withdraw what she has had up my cunt. I am curious to catch a glimpse of this pleasure-giving device, expecting – or perhaps hoping – to see a delicate little dildo. One that Ursula found useful to have on her should the opportunity for passion present itself unexpectedly. One like those fake bones that dog-owners buy for their pets. Peach-coloured with FIDO picked out in raised letters. They have them on sale in the 'Miscellaneous Welcome Presents' at Emrys Powell's Eager To Please store in Pontycymmer, up the Garw Valley. A bonus spot for anyone who enjoys a browse, with all kinds of bargains to be bought. But I don't imagine that Ursula would have bought hers at the Eager To Please. If anyone like Ursula ever appeared in Pontycymmer which shelters a dark, dusty, primitive coalmining community, steeped in the traditions of the non-conformist chapel, there would be widespread pandemonium. She would probably be eulogised as an angel, with her spectacular golden hair. Or else burnt in a secret ceremony at the top of the coal shaft, as a witch.

I think that she is both.

As I crane around (I am still arse in the air and am dreading the spine-cracking process of straightening up) to see what it is, I cannot believe that what has happened has really taken place. But I watch as Ursula sniffs at her glistening fingers, her middle and fore, which appear glued together.

'Mm, mm, ambroisa,' she says in the throaty growl. Then, to the fascination of Siriol and myself, she avidly begins to lick them.

Chapter 12

Saul Polanski is tall. Tall and superby built. Like a giant. Beside him I feel as Mavis must feel with everyone that she meets. Small and delicate, there to be taken care of, and vulnerable. It's not a sensation that I have ever experienced before. Even when I was much younger, with Zeus Bowen, when I was thirteen I still felt mature and wise. As if I were the adult. This man is a colossus. He looks like a Michelangelo's David. It's my guess that he has been practising muscle-building exercises since the age of four. But when I ask him he simply shrugs. 'This is the way we're all built where I come from.'

I inwardly swoon at the sound of the voice. It starts up from his navel – or should I be honest and say from the balls? It is the ballsiest voice that I've ever heard. It's the male equivalent of Ursula's husky drawl. When I've time to myself I must start working on my vocal chords, see if I can't manufacture the same sort of knock-'em-in-the-aisles, kick-'em-in-the goolies and kiss-'em-in-the-chops voice of my own. It's simply a matter of lowering the key several octaves. That and a life-time of tobacco and hard liquor. I've got a lot of catching up to do.

'And where do you come from?' I hear myself asking, a mixture of the arch and the minx. Christ, I sound like that silly Southern belle, that twerp Scarlett O'Hara that Siriol and I saw recently in the re-run of an oldie called *Gone With The Wind*. What a load of baloney that was! And here I am employing the same set of tricks, what's known in the trade as womanly wiles. Me, Boadicea Jones, of all people! I can only pray that Siriol's not listening, the girl that I've lectured so often in the past for letting the side down, the feminist front.

And it's not as if Saul Polanski is anywhere near as handsome as Boyo. I'm not merely reacting to masculine beauty, I'm too used to that in my own home. In fact, taken feature for feature, there is something amiss with this giant's face. The mouth which dominates the whole is too generous, much too loose in the lower lip, too greedy and self-indulgent. I haven't yet seen him eat, not seen him demolish a plate of food. That'll be something worth waiting for. He must eat like a horse to keep this physique on the road. It's a good job Mrs Pugh is not with us to complain. Yet another criticism to be levelled against the Yanks.

For Saul Polanski is an American. But his forebears hail from Poland, he explains, and yesterday it was the Polish-Welsh part of the family that he was tracking down in Cardiff. But Saul Polanski regards himself now, with his permanent residence in L.A., as a product of California.

'You'll like Los Angeles, Boadicea,' he's saying to me. To me! *You'll like Los Angeles!* Just taking it for granted that that's where I'll be going! But how? And who with? *And when – for Christ's sake?*

'Yes,' I reply, my eyes glowing, 'I've always planned to visit Hollywood. In my opinion it's as important, culturally speaking, as the Parthenon, Giotto's frescoes, St Mark's Sqare in Venice, The Sistine Chapel, the Pompidou Centre in Paris –'

'Bullshit!' The force of his comment causes the two straws in my Harvey Wallbanger to keel over. I stare at them in distress. We've reached the point in the evening when a mishap such as this can reduce me to sudden tears. I feel that everything has got a little bit out of hand. From being madly in love with Saul Polanski, certain that we were going to elope before dawn and live happily ever after, I now am not even sure whether I like him. Sure I'm still reacting madly to the thrill of the voice and if I concentrate hard I can just about hang onto the undeniable draw of that louche lower lip. But as to whether we're getting on together – as to whether this is going to be the romance of the century – I think that this time I've really blown it.

It's the fault of that bitch Ursula.

Since our encounter in the ladies lavatory, I feel as if I've been drained of my previous drive. I can't concentrate on anything, least of all what people are saying all around me. I've lost focus, that's what it is. All I can think about is the feel of those thrusting fingers. And my condition is not helped by the glimpses I keep getting of Ursula's dimples across the crowded bar. Despite myself and my desire, which I mean to direct solely towards Saul Polanski, I am all too conscious of Ursula's husky laugh drifting across at me. I don't want to be this drawn by her, there doesn't seem space in my life for such complications. If I could choose what to do now I'd just go quietly home to bed with Siriol and stay awake until the dawn broke, discussing it all. But I am having to cope with everything on my own. Siriol is dancing with Boyo, and has been for the last three numbers. Now the both of them have linked up with Mavis and Darren, and are involved in an intricate routine of their own invention.

I glance up at Saul, it's one of the things I do like about him – the having to look up. His expression is still one of withering contempt for my trite display of intellect, but I forge on nevertheless. It seems I can do little to engage his interest, erotic or otherwise, so what the hell ...

'What do you think of my sister?' I point over to the dance-floor. 'She's gorgeous, isn't she?' I state this as a matter of fact, not a question of debate. For there is no denying that Mavis is an arresting vision at this moment. In my antique wedding dress, ripped beyond recognition (one sleeve has completely disappeared, the bodice a mass of holes where the fabric has rotted away rather than bear the weight of her bosom), Mavis looks an exotic gypsy. Her black hair has broken loose of the forties style which she tried to impose on it before we left the house. Any make-up has long since become blurred and smudged in the heat of this place and the shiny, sweaty effect is more becoming than any application of cosmetic could be. I'd never seen her looking more ravishing.

Saul Polanski swings around to stare at the group of them. Siriol has just whispered something to Boyo, who throws back his head in guffaws of appreciation. He and Mavis could be twins, Boyo is wearing a white shirt undone to the navel. As he gyrates the gold chains on his dark torso catch the light. Another gypsy. Just a question which sex you prefer. I follow the line of Saul Polanski's vision to see who he has chosen to look at.

His eyes are firmly fixed on my brother.

Chapter 13

Mrs Pugh has called in to say her farewells before leaving with 'Haemmoroid' Hughes for the station. At this moment they are waiting for the station taxi to arrive: though we are within walking distance of the railway terminus old 'Haemmoroid' can't manage the cases.

'Carrying too much backways,' I whisper to Siriol. Mavis overhears and gives me a shove. I nearly drop the loaded tray that I'm carrying. We are all of us dreadfully ill after too much drinking. But I am more up to the mark than anyone else. The only one who can face them in the dining room. Even Siriol, who can usually be counted on to turn up trumps on the morning after our puerile school dances, where cider is served to sixth formers, even she is devastated this morning. She has agreed to carry food as far as the dining-room door, but she has point blank refused to actually face people. So I am having to take my own tray in, serve the contents to the guests, run back to the hall-way corridor where she is waiting with hers and then serve that all again myself. The same procedure goes on with the discarded dishes. I am dizzy with it all.

The last thing we need this morning is Mrs Pugh spreading sentiment and high emotion. But even so we all obediently line up to be kissed and hugged. My turn comes last, and it's for me that she has saved especial embraces. I'm suffocated by the overwhelming smell of camphor balls and lavender bags clinging to her clothing. It brings back appalling memories of chapel. But at the same time I feel moved. It seems to me that what I'm embracing here is the final link with my childhood. While I am aware that worse will come when it's time to bid Blodwen farewell, this is a painful rehearsal for that last cruel wrench. And it's not that I am the only one who is suffering from it. I'm affected most of all by the poignancy of those that I'm leaving behind. I've got everything before me. They are being left with nothing.

I am suddenly incapacitated by the most abject pity and to my horror, held in the camphorous prison of Mrs Pugh's embrace, I burst into childish tears. The rest turn away out of embarrassment, or amusement. I think Siriol believes that I am putting it on, later on she will probably congratulate me on my acting. But I am mystified by my reaction. All I can think is that my hangover has reduced me to a particularly emotional state. Mrs Pugh is very well satisfied. I have made her day.

'There, there, my little love,' she is crooning, stroking my shaking shoulders. 'That's it, let it all out, have a good old weep. I'll be back though, you'll see – I'm not going for good. You haven't seen the last of me by a long chalk!'

When she says that I realise for the first time that she has no intention of returning. That her devious plan is to marry old 'Haemmoroid' and live happily ever after, as the others have kept telling me. And at that a rush of genuine warmth causes me to crush the old harridan closely to me. It is the only time in my life that I have harboured any affection for her. Is this to be the summer of my softening?

But now she's gone. We have all collapsed onto various kitchen chairs and are drinking Boyo's specially brewed black coffee instead of the instant stuff that we usually make do with. This treat is in Saul Polanski's honour, but he is not partaking with us. He is still in bed. Boyo has just taken his breakfast up to him on a tray. Very nice indeed for some! Now he's out of the room I am able to put my thoughts into words, thoughts that have been bothering me since last night.

'Do you think,' I say in a stage whisper, 'that Saul Polanski is a gay person?'

'I think he has masses of sexual magnetism, but he's not particularly jolly, is he?' Siriol says innocently.

I look at her to see if she's deliberately misunderstanding me. Mavis is blinking in my direction, I think she has got the message.

'Are you being deliberately dense, Siriol?'

'Oh!' Comprehension slowly dawns in her eyes. 'I see what you mean. *Gay* – is Saul a pooftah? Well now, I wouldn't be surprised. I should think he has everything, wouldn't you – man, woman and beast? Just as well you don't have a cat and a canary in the house,' she gives a raucous gurgle, 'otherwise you'd probably catch him screwing them too.'

I look at Mavis to see what she thinks. She's nodding in agreement, how much less of a prude she has become since Siriol has been staying with us. But I am amazed by her next words.

'Yes, I think so too. I wouldn't be at all surprised if he weren't a fist fucker. You know – the fist fuckers of California.' She bursts out laughing. 'Your faces! Haven't you heard about them? I read this article about how they introduce their fists up each other's anus's.'

'What, both at the same time?' I am aghast and fascinated.

'One at a time. And then the trick is to watch the fingers and knuckles moving around in the stomach.' Mavis looks pleased with herself at having been in the rare position of enlightening us. Especially me, since traditionally I am the one who knows all these things.

'Ugh!' Siriol shudders. 'I'm not trying it.'

'No-one's asking you, Siriol,' I said. 'Go on, Mavis, get on with it.'

'That's all I know.'

'And you think he may be one?' I ruminate on this. 'I wouldn't like one of his fists up my arse, I must say. My sphincter is shrinking at the mere thought of it.' I wriggle on my chair, feeling suddenly raw and vulnerable in that certain spot. 'He does make blue movies, he was telling me last night, so I suppose he has to go along with all the latest sexual trends.'

'Blue movies! How thrilling!' Siriol's eyes are shining. 'Does he perform in them or does he direct them?'

'From what I could gather he produces them now, but I think he has directed them – and performed in them too, in his time. But he claimed that his cock's not up to much. The size of his body goes against him, he says that the best people for pornographic photographs and films are those on the small size with spectacular dongs. Being small makes the tool appear that much larger. His is just average apparently, but dwarfed by the rest of him –'

'What's dwarfed by the rest of him, eh?' Boyo creeps up behind my chair and puts his hands over my eyes, playfully, as he used to do. There hasn't been much intimacy between Boyo and myself since these various people have introduced themselves into the family. Not that the emotion we have for each other has altered. Feeling his firm hands over my face I immediately lean my head back against him. It hits his hard stomach.

'We're talking about the size of Saul's tool,' I purr.

'Ah! What do you want to know about it? – I can probably help you there.' His voice is as casual as anything.

'Christ, Boyo!' I state the unspoken surprise on the faces of the others, Siriol's and Mavis's. Boyo has let his hands slip away from my eyes so that I can see once again.

'Well you must have guessed that, surely, little sister. You're the clever one around here.' He straddles the spare kitchen chair and smiles the familiar heart-melting smile. I wonder who seduced whom of the two of them.

'Are you both exclusively homosexual, Boyo?' I hear myself saying, barely able to tear my eyes from Siriol's tragic expression, controlling a chortling spiral of laughter from escaping at the same time. He simply shrugs off my question.

113

'Who is exclusively anything these days, Boadicea darling?'

'Exactly!' Mavis has decided to say something.

The silence that follows has no uneasiness, but if poor old Blodwen, stuffy Blodwen, were here now I wouldn't reveal what I am about to reveal.

'I had a homosexual encounter of my own last night. Didn't I, Siriol?'

Siriol's eyes roll. 'I'll say!'

We grin conspiratorially at each other. 'Orgasms all round!' I can't help it, I start laughing at the astounded expression on Boyo's face. Mavis's is a little harder to fathom. 'Naughty goings-on at the No Name. In the ladies' lavatory to be absolutely precise.'

'Ursula!'

'Right, Boyo, in one. Ursula, t'was Ursula, who did the dirty deed!' I burst into song at this point, high soprano. They put their hands over their ears, but it's hard for me to suppress my *joie de vivre*. Even this morning with my system racked by the ravages of alcohol. Am I recovering from Zeus Bowen after all?

Boyo is scowling. 'That bitch Ursula propositioned you in the ladies lavatory? I knew she'd be up to something, she can never resist a bit of fresh. And her awful girl-friend wasn't there at the beginning to keep an eye on her. I s'pose that's when it happened. Where did she want you to meet her? Come on, I need to know, Boadicea.' He is glaring angrily at me. The skin at the back of my neck begins to tingle. I think my big brother is jealous. I take a discarded triangle of cold toast from the kitchen table, from a small pile which will later be ground down to make bread crumbs, and I spread it liberally with butter and then marmalade. This will infuriate Mavis and Boyo who have to watch every single calorie like hawks. It drives them mad that I can eat whatever I like without the fear of putting on an ounce of weight. I take a big bite before I drop my beautiful bombshell.

'We did it there on the spot, Boyo. There was no need to meet later anywhere. She got it over and done with in ... oh, how long would you say Ursula took to make me come,

Siriol? I'd have said five minutes from start to finish, wouldn't you?' I give a self-satisfied grin.

The taste of salted Welsh butter congealing with Cooper's Chunky Marmalade is the final memory I have before losing consciousness.

Chapter 14

I am lying in bed dozing, drifting in and out of a hallucinatory sleep. I'm not dreaming exactly and yet all the familiar objects in my bedroom have assumed a mysterious presence. The plaster angel that I begged to be given me from my mother's grave in the cemetery, which as a child I firmly believed to be picking its nose, seems reproachful in its pose of petrified admonishment. The raised finger, the bowed head, the half-open mouth conspire towards this cautionary attitude. I must control my behaviour in future, it seems to be saying.

It's time for the angel to go.

I move my head, an excruciating pain leaps over my scalp to remind me of the bizarre event which has brought me to my bed at such an hour of the day. The curtain is drawn but glimmering sunshine leaks through which means that it is around noon. It's then that this bedroom of mine begins to fall into shadow. A deliberate choice of mine that, to take the side of the house that wakes up to the sun, starting the day right. Not that it has had much of a favourable influence on this morning. There is someone in this room with me, I can sense that there is, but I can't rouse my reeling senses sufficiently to establish who it is. But I struggle to speak.

'Hello,' I quaver, my eyelids fluttering. A large shape looms into focus.

'Hello, kid. How're you feeling?' The large shape is Boyo.

'Boyo.' I stretch out my arms, they are bare to my surprise. Beneath this duvet I must be naked yet I have no recollection of being relieved of my clothes. Did my brother undress me, I wonder?

'Bo,' he is whispering softly and taking me in his arms. He is lifting me gently from the pillow and cradling me, rocking me to and fro like one would with a little baby. But I'm not a little baby. I am a fully grown young person, precocious for my age, mature beyond my years. Should I perhaps remind him of that?

'How's the head?' he continues to whisper, crooning the words into my ear. His warm breath tickles the skin on my neck. I press closer to him so that I shan't be able to feel it, and as I do so his own grip tightens on me.

My head is thumping in one specific spot. I know without touching that I must have a colossal lump there. But at this moment I don't have any desire to check. It's nice being held by Boyo, he's so solid and firm to the touch. It must be like this when survivors at sea find something to cling to in the giddying swell of tempestuous waves. As long as I'm hanging on to him I shall feel safe. But we must talk of the blow to my head which has incapacitated me, I know that. I wait for him to bring up the subject, though I want him to understand that I don't mind talking about it myself.

'Boyo ...'

'Shush, shush,' he murmurs into my short hair, stroking the bare skin of my shoulder. And I sigh and smile to myself, engulfed in a rush of tenderness for him, kissing the soft hairiness of his beard. And remember the dreadful fury on his face as I disclosed the absolute about Ursula and me in the ladies' lavatory. Was it too brutal a confession? Had I let my coarseness get the better of me? I snuggle closer still against my big brother.

'Boyo,' I begin again. But this time he silences me with his mouth on mine. Our first carnal kiss. And me too dazed and dopey to register the added piquancy of it being incestuous. Strange how little I worry about this man, who now is

117

earnestly and determinedly making the most marvellous love to me, being my own flesh and blood. We melt into each other, I seem to hover above myself watching the tableau, the slow-motion slide of it all. That first kiss which seems to go on and on, tongues lashing like newts in a storm. And then both of us moving with these same tongues forking small darts of lust over each other's torsos. Me with my limp fingers momentarily strong, tearing away at the buttons on his shirt, eager to get at him. Then rubbing my tough, tiny breasts against his hairy chest – like a young animal with its mother.

And I feel like an animal. God in heaven – do I not! I can't think of anything in the whole world, now and forever, amen, besides aching for his fine, stiff penis inside me. It's mine and I want it. My piece of flesh, meant for me. I view it with as much pride of possession as if it were attached to my person.

Now it is.

It wasn't me who unzipped Boyo's leather trousers – or was it? Minutes are scudding past as swiftly as summer clouds in the sky. The sort that Zeus and I used to take such delight in when we lay together in our secret place in the sand dunes. So that all is confused as to who is doing what to whom. But I shall remember the jack-in-the-box action of his upright cock springing to attention as long as I live. Freed from the restrictions of a particularly fetching deep purple pair of underpants, cut on the lines of my G-string, there was no knowing where that lively tool of his would wander. Jerking and bobbing, head in the air, all over the place. Searching for a warm spot to snuggle into. Aiming unerringly to that fiery nest between my legs, urging me closer and closer until we were touching.

'Oh, Boadicea, my beautiful Bo,' Boyo is groaning against my mouth, trying as hard as he knows how to hold back.

But I press on ruthlessly, unable to exert any moral control, not wanting to examine the position we are in. I scoop his genitals into my shaky fingers, dizzy with desire, and steadying myself against his trunk I bend my head and begin tongue-ing my handful. The pain in my head recedes now as I get

118

carried away by what I'm doing. There is a faint saltiness in my mouth, a taste of sweet and sour milkiness lining my tongue. I can smell a lingering of bath soap on the baby-soft pubic hair that is invading my nostrils. I take the tip of my brother's circumcised penis between my tingling lips and start sucking slowly around the rim of it. Gently at first as if I'm licking an ice-cream, around and around. There is no sound at all from Boyo, not so much as a murmur. But I don't need to look up to see whether he is enjoying it. Now and then a fresh rush of blood engorges his cock to even greater proportions. If a sausage manufacturer were in charge of these proceedings he would call a halt, for fear of bursting the boundaries, breaking out through the enclosing skin. I am holding tightly onto the base of this massive shaft and have begun to rub up and down, up and down, but just gently as I'm licking the tip. There is no need to rush things. I feel that I have all the time in the world, after all – haven't I waited almost eighteen years for this!

Now stealthily I bring my other hand into play. Boyo seems to have left this planet, floated off into space. I can barely hear him breathing, though he is taking air in a peculiarly rapid and shallow fashion. Like a puppy does when it's excited. And I have no wish to distract him. It's just that I am in considerable need of attention myself. If someone – or something – doesn't touch my seething snatch in a second I think I shall go mad!

So I slide my hand down, down there between my legs, catching the nub of my clitoris against my fore-finger and begin frantically rubbing against it. I don't intend it to be this energetic, but I underestimated my need. And what I'm doing now has exacerbated this need. I am going to have to mount my big brother.

In preparation for this act of rape, I force my mouth down on his huge erection. As far as it will go. And I give it a last, final suck. I'm drawing my cheeks in and holding my breath, and my mouth is swimming with saliva. And I'm all the while rolling my tongue around to keep the action on the move. And then I swiftly draw back, leaving the soaking wet wand bravely steaming on its own. Cruel me!

The perfect pillar upon which to impale myself.

But I hadn't reckoned with Boyo's fervent participation. The very second of entry arouses him from the sensual trance which he had succumbed to. His return to consciousness is immediate, and enthusiastically amorous. It is as if he is surprised to find me there, as if he is more used to having his cock sucked than anything else. That all he has to do is lay back and enjoy it. Which might be the case if what he claimed of his homosexuality is true. But this is a different game altogether, the one that we're playing now. I watch his face, the delight that spreads over it like a smile. The loving look in his beautiful pale eyes, two blue mirrors reflecting my own.

'Hello, there.' I ease myself down onto him, forcing the pace. Bearing the pain that I'm having to endure in accommodating his width – and length. This is the hugest prick that's pleasured me. And it is pleasure too, despite the pain, now throbbing at both ends of my person, because my head has started to play up again. When this is all over I shall plead for a pain killer. But only to deaden the topmost part of me. I shall want to hang onto the sensations currently wracking my cunt.

Despite the intensity of the sexual flow I am already aware of the approaching end and the sadness which will inevitably lace the exhilaration I shall feel. I don't want to consider how either of us will regard the other when it's over. I don't ever want it to end.

I ease myself up again, skilfully to the topmost tip. I hear Boyo catching his breath fearing that I shall lose him altogether, let my precious prize slip right out of my cunt's grasp. But I am more practised than that, as he must be realising. He is not being fucked by an amateur!

Ten, twenty, perhaps more times I tease him this way. Until he is gritting his teeth in an effort to stop himself coming.

'Enough,' I grin, sitting back on my heels, looking down on his cock. It looks as if it's sprouting straight from my cunt. Joining the two of us together.

'A family tie,' I say pointing at it. 'Look!'

He raises his arms towards me and takes my lowered face between his hands. 'Don't,' his voice is hoarse and emotional, with a crack in it like a sob. 'Don't remind me, Bo. Bo, my love.'

I'm moved by the way he's said that. I love Boyo, I have always loved him as a brother, and I am upset at the thought of him ever suffering. Very upset. It makes me want to protect him in a motherly way, nothing to do with the loving between us at this very moment. But at the same time I can't possibly condone any suffering brought about by guilt, Christian guilt. My conscience is unsullied by ridiculous theories of right and wrong over what we are enjoying. My sexual ardour cools at the thought that I may have to re-educate Boyo's attitude towards incest. That the conventional concept is merely there to be challenged by the individual. But instead of expounding my clearly-defined theories on the topic, I bend forward and kiss my brother passionately on one nipple. Then I engineer it that I am beneath him. The good old missionary position. I shall soon cheer him up now.

But we finish on the side, facing each other. Able to gaze for an eternity at each other's faces. I trace around the edge of his marvellous mouth with my fingertips, moving my body rhythmically down below. His thighs, his hips, his about-to-come cock are lodged between my limbs. It is comfortable this way, a favourite with Zeus Bowen. He liked it because it was easier to talk and keep a contact going, that's what he said. That the intimacy of intense love-making created a distance between partners. That the force of their individual passion carried one away from the other. He was very hot on that. And so we would deliberately chat in the middle of things, to force our deep fondness for each other to mingle with the strength of the desire. It's only now that I'm beginning to appreciate what an advantage it will prove to have been taught the refinements of love by a poet.

And the brutality of betrayal.

'This is so lovely,' I murmur to Boyo, steadily responding to his thrusts. He smiles tenderly at me, continuing the action.

121

'How's the lump, kid?'

I smile back at him. 'Oh – the lump!' My voice is euphoric. 'It's the largest lump that I've ever had. I didn't know that they made lumps like this one!' And I start moving a pace faster.

'Well,' he responds by moving faster too. 'Mavis landed you a pretty firm whack with that wooden tray. We were afraid that you'd passed out for good.'

Chapter 15

'One more week to my eighteenth birthday. Two more days to our "A" level examination results. And the rest of today to live through in agony, rushing every few minutes to the lavatory to see whether or not I sight blood. Great!'

My periods are three days late.

Siriol nods philosophically. 'It does all seem to be coming together, I agree. But let's be more objective. The birthday will be nice, you'll have a terrific beach party – midnight bathing in the nude, all that sort of thing. You and Boyo will be able to slope off in the dark together and get up to your usual tricks. The "A" level results will be a piece of cake too, just heap greater glories on your head. And as to the other thing – what do you bet that you'll have come on by this time tomorrow?'

'Thanks.' I refuse to be fobbed off in this flip manner. 'But if I haven't come on by this time tomorrow, or any other morrow before the other two events, then there's not going to be cause for celebration. Midnight bathing in the nude is not an activity you're very much drawn to when you're puking your ring up with morning sickness. And as for receiving further academic honours, they're not going to do me much good if I can't put them to use. I'm not sure what the position is regarding pregnant undergraduates at Balliol – bloody nil, I should think.'

'You could ring and enquire, Bo.' Siriol looks at me doubtfully. 'Or couldn't you?'

I shake my head, touching her kindly on the shoulder. Poor friend, she's only trying to be helpful.

'More to the point, Siriol, what do you think of my chances as an unmarried mother, of taking over from Margaret Thatcher as the next female Prime Minister? That, as you know, is my main aim in life.'

'Well,' she clears her throat, 'let me think about it carefully. It could endear you to the nation, might catch the women's votes. It shows an independent streak, doesn't it? You'd have to come clean about it from the very start, otherwise your political opponents could make some heavy ammunition out of it if you'd tried to hide the fact and then they found out. British politics now are not what they used to be. They've taken their cue from the Americans now and fight very dirty.'

She's a bore, poor old Siriol when she expounds her views on changing aspects in the established order of public behaviour and life in Great Britain. It's what comes of having taken her 'A' level sociology course too seriously. I'm of the lurking suspicion that Siriol will fail in this subject, for simply parroting what she reads in the textbooks. Instead of forming imaginative and original opinions of her own. But I say, 'Mm,' nevertheless. She can get overly sensitive if I ignore her serious side, like many rather sweet but stupid people. And she's been an invaluable friend these last few weeks, I have to say that. I don't really know how I would have managed without her help, regarding Boyo and me, I mean.

'I could always get rid of it, the foetus.' I look down at my stomach, as flat as an ironing board. It is a novel idea, the thought that inside there I may be harbouring a baby. Boyo's baby. I am at least certain of that. The first month, since I began menstruating and having sex, that I can say with absolute conviction that I know who the father of my child would be. I've never been faced with this problem before, but if I had then I would have been forced to draw up a whole list of possibles. It surprises me to think of how many different fucks I would whizz through in any one month. I haven't gone short on sex even with just one lover. Boyo has been quite enough for me.

'You probably would, wouldn't you, Bo? Most girls in your position would get rid of it – but then you are not representative, so I never take it for granted that you'd take the obvious course.'

Something about the way Siriol said this makes me grin. I think it's her air of resigned acceptance, as if she's known me for a very, very long time. But still tolerates all my impossible peculiarities. And she doesn't bear me any malice over taking over Boyo, despite having admitted that she was half in love with him herself. But then she does have Mavis to take her mind off her loss. We are now a thoroughly depraved household.

It's nice seeing Mavis and Siriol together, their gentleness together and the affection that Mavis displays towards Siriol is a help to Boyo, regarding me. But he is still wracked with conscience over the situation, terrified that we are going to be found out. Discovered living in sin, is how he put it. As if we haven't spent all our lives eating and sleeping under the same roof. Though not sleeping together.

It is my idea, the sleeping together. It's the most marvellous way of celebrating another person's body that I have experienced. It's the very first time that I've done it, it beats stand-up, spin-off screws into a cocked hat. If that's the right expression! I realise that my previous way of snatching sex wherever and whenever I could was a sacrilege. However satisfying it seemed at the time, in retrospect it was simply a light snack. Sleeping with a lover for the entire night is a banquet. That first night Boyo and I made love six times.

Saul Polanski has gone, he left the same day that I was recovering from the blow to my scalp that Mavis had delivered. She and I have still not discussed that extraordinary incident. Perhaps it isn't that odd. We've both had too much on our minds since then. I have had to rely on Siriol to recount the subsequent happenings, satisfyingly embroidered with all the details.

'You went out like a light, Bo. Just crumpled down in the chair and slid onto the floor before any of us could catch you. It was amazing, the whole thing! I couldn't move, honestly. I think it was because I was hypnotised by Mavis. She looked like a witch, all white in the face, with that tray still held up high in the air. I got the impression that if you hadn't slipped down as you did, she would just have gone on crashing it down on your head. Terrifying. As if she was possessed by demons, out of her head. We've talked about it since, she and I.' Here Siriol had given a sly, secret smile. 'And it seems to me that you had just touched on a sensitive area. You didn't know, did you, that Mavis had been living with a girl in Bristol for the past year?'

'I knew she was sharing with a flatmate, yes.'

'Ah, but you had no idea of the actual relationship.'

'You mean –'

'Right. But it's all over now. Mavis came home and found her girl-friend with someone else. Big scene, usual fight, and now Mavis is left on her own.'

'Oh, dear!' I stared at Siriol. 'She's never mentioned anything of all that. Poor Mavis. I thought she was keen to get tied up with one of these fearful twerps down here, that estate agent with the swish car.'

'Geraint Thomas. Lotus Elan.' Siriol prompted me.

'That's the one. His father's big in Bangor.'

'She despises them all in this one-eyed town and who wouldn't. You won't catch me hanging around here after this summer.' Siriol smiled her sly smile again. It made me wonder what plans she had. Perhaps the training college plan would be chucked out of the window.

'But she's kept coming back here every summer since she left home.' I objected. 'She can't have loathed it that much.'

'A matter of conscience. Feeling indebted to Blodwen more than anything. The running around with the locals has been simply a smoke-screen. She could hardly have let you know which way her leanings really lay, could she?' Siriol said, impassioned. Mavis had really enslaved her.

'She gave me a fair enough indication,' I say, not liking the feeling of being left out in the cold. Unable to have sensed that my sister's life was so much more complex that I could have imagined.

'Touching your tits!' Siriol had given a short laugh. 'That was nothing. You should see the things that we do together. Honestly Bo, I know that you're not the best person for me to extol the delights of lesbian love to, obsessed with Boyo as you are, but I've had more orgasms with Mavis, real mind-shattering ones, than anything I've experienced with boys.'

'Well, yes, *boys*!' I'd scoffed scornfully. '*Boys*!' Then I remembered that as far as Siriol knew, the only sex I'd had was with an unknown boy, whilst she was away in France. Apart from Boyo. And Ursula.

'Anyway,' I hurried on, 'I'm not completely inexperienced in the ways and the wiles and the sexual expertise of women, if you recall, Siriol. What about Ursula?'

She wasn't thrown by that. Quite the reverse.

'Well to tell you the truth, if I hadn't got so excited by seeing what Ursula did to you that night,' she put her hand in an involuntary action between her thighs as if re-living the thrill of the occasion, 'I would have been shocked or too shy, or something ridiculous like that, when Mavis made that first overture to me. Actually it wasn't even an overture. After Boyo carried you to your bedroom leaving me to calm Mavis down – she was horrified by what she'd done when she recovered her senses a little – I was just comforting her. That's how it started, me holding her to me, just an arm around her shoulder, that sort of thing ...'

'Yes, that's how it started with Boyo and me,' I sighed pleasurably. 'Just with an arm around a shoulder.'

'Then what?' Siriol looked expectantly into my face.

'No, you say. You say what happened with you and Mavis. I have to have time to word mine properly otherwise I won't do it justice – the idyllic part, I mean.'

Siriol adores these sort of conversations, as I have come to do. But with this worry about periods I'm finding it hard to fling myself into the spirit of the thing. This morning we had another cryptic card from Blodwen. It seems as if she has no intention of ever coming home! Not that anyone here is anxious that she should return. That really would upset the apple-cart!

'Do you think you should tell Boyo, Bo?' Siriol is asking solicitously. 'You like to share everything with him. It might make you feel better about it.'

'Absolutely not, Siriol!' I am adamant. 'And I'll *kill* you if you so much as breathe a word to Mavis.'

There is a silence. Siriol is pulling at a tiny piece of loose skin at the side of one of her finger-nails.

'Siriol – you cunt! You've told Mavis already!' I stare at her quivering mouth.

'Well, it's only Mavis – she is your sister.' Her pale face is scarlet with confusion. This is a new turn of events. Neither of us has ever betrayed a confidence. Not since we were eleven and beginning to be good friends. The end of an era, one more sign that my childhood is splintering apart.

'And Boyo is my brother. So?' I mean to look at her coldly for her treachery. Shall I let on about having had it off with her brother-in-law on the day of his wedding to her Glenis? Shall I tell her about the foreign exchange student, the one she thought had given her the pox? Shall I shock her with the saga of her hero, Zeus Bowen? But I don't do anything at all. I don't even look at her coldly. For whilst we're sitting here on this cliff, overlooking the bay with a nippy autumnal wind ruffling our skin, I feel a gushing warmth down in my cunt. I clutch her arm.

'Cross your fingers, Siriol – I think something's happening!' At my words there's another rush. I'm wearing a pair of my tightest trousers. A pin-striped pair of men's trousers, the sort that solicitors wear, and old-fashioned bank managers who ignore all the television commercials aimed at updating the image of banks. 'Jesus, Siriol,' I moan. 'I don't want to ruin this pair of pants, they're the ones I got from Bethesda Chapel "Bring and Buy". Keep cover while I make sure what this leak looks like.'

'Bound to be blood.' Siriol smirks in her self-satisfied manner, purposely to irritate me at this time of great drama. 'Which means that I win my bet.'

But I'm not bothering with bets now. I'm down on my knees and tugging at these trousers. It takes me five minutes to even get the bastards on! Whoever owned the fuckers must have been built like Jack Sprat, because there are few hips that are narrower than mine. Given the length of leg. Now they're down and I'm crouching down amongst the gorse.

'Look – look at that, Siriol!' I'm pointing triumphantly at the scarlet gout of blood staining my white gusset. She hugs me with the same excitement that I'm feeling.

'A future again, Siriol! That's what that means!'

'The Premiership. Boadicea!' Siriol's eyes are shining, caught up in the mood of the moment. That's what I appreciate about her. The readiness to adapt. Not everyone has the capacity to do that.

'Here goes then!' I tear off the wrapping from the Tampax that I have in my shoulder-bag. One that I've been carrying around with me in readiness for this very event. And I take aim at my sticky red hole.

'Here I am, corked up like vintage wine.'

'Port wine!' screams Siriol into the wind. And we throw back our heads and start singing at the top of our voices. The sound of lunatic angels.

Chapter 16

Siriol has failed every one of her examinations. I have passed with flying colours, an 'A' in each subject. It's difficult to sympathise with the poor girl when people, everywhere we go, keep rushing up to congratulate me. Now I regret having done so well. If I nonchalantly dismiss my success as a mere nothing, something anyone can achieve, it only makes her own failure appear even more abject. And to make matters worse her parents are insisting that she return to school to re-sit the whole thing all over again.

'I can't go back to that bloody awful place can I, Bo? No-one can go on being a schoolgirl at my age!' She appeals to me.

'Well,' I console her, 'you're eighteen, you can do what you like now. You're not under your parents' jurisdiction any more.'

'No,' she says bleakly, staring into space. The only thing that arouses her from the torpor is the thought of Mavis and their love affair. Often I come into the room to catch them cuddling, or just sitting closely together holding hands. Once, when I entered stealthily and unannounced – not meaning to syp – I caught them in an act of intimacy.

Mavis was lying back in an armchair, her button-through

ummer dress open all the way down. It's white, a crisp, stiff
cotton cut like a sheath, with broad shoulder-straps and no
sleeves. She always looks ravishing in this particular dress.
It's not new. She's had it for years, wearing it at first as
something to put on for special occasions only. Now she just
wears it around the house. Giving us pleasure, and many of the
male guests apoplexia. Mavis could seduce anything in that
dress. Beneath it she was wearing nothing but a pair of brief
bikini pants, also white. These were no longer covering her
pubis, they were down around one ankle, hanging half-on and
half-off her delicate foot hovering in the air over the side of
the chair. Siriol was kneeling between her legs earnestly
sucking her off. But at the same time she was managing to
twiddle Mavis's nipples up above. She looked like a praying
mantis.

I was spellbound by the scene. It was like watching the sex
films in the cinema downtown that I enjoy sneaking off to on
my own so much. Once Zeus Bowen and I really played with
fire by meeting inside this sleazy cinema. His idea, not mine.
We didn't dream that we'd be seen by anyone we knew, and
we weren't either but it was a bloody close shave. In front
of us, just six or seven rows ahead was Williams the Dairy.
That's old Williams the Dairy!' I'd whispered, horrified, to
Zeus. 'So it is,' he'd replied. 'Good on the old bugger – more
strength to his elbow!' Williams hadn't seen us, he was too interested in the screen. The film featured an actress with enor-
mous mammaries who smothered her lovers to death with her
tits. The posters claimed that this leading lady, Chesty Morgan,
measured 63-24-36. Whether this unlikely statistic was true
we couldn't tell, but she was certainly top-heavy. And the big
things kept getting dreadfully in the way. In one scene where
she was taking a bath the water overflowed when she lowered
them in. And when she started lathering her cleavage she
lost the bar of soap in between, such that she had to arise,
dripping like a Venus at the Fountain to fetch herself a fresh
tablet from the shelf. A way to get all the men in the audience
going.

It certainly got Zeus going. As soon as we'd sat down he

131

drew my hand to his erection. He wanted me to jerk him off there in the dark. All the rows of seats were rocking rhythmically together. And I realised that practically every chap in the cinema was wanking, pulling himself off over those colossal titties of Chesty Morgan. When I got home I sighed at my own impoverished pair. If I hadn't been so sure of my sexual identity and pulling power I might have felt thoroughly demoralised. As it was I just shrugged it off. Hadn't Zeus Bowen Wales's greatest contemporary poet, just complimented me on my magnificent hand-job? A girl didn't have to have huge knockers to get ahead – anyway, Chesty Morgan had a hell of a problem with stretch marks.

This scene between Mavis and Siriol wasn't like that film which relied on the grotesque for its appeal. Members of the audience were laughing out loud, from embarrassment as much as anything. No audience would laugh at what I was watching. And I was watching it, I couldn't tear myself away. I knew perfectly well that I should have tip-toed to another part of the house. But I wouldn't have been able to get this picture out of my mind. The way Mavis was pressing Siriol's silky head down harder against her cunt, a hand enclosing each side of the head and moving it slightly up and down, then from side to side. She was moaning very softly, her beautiful lips slightly apart and swollen. Swollen the way that Boyo's become fuller when we are in the full flush of our passionate sessions.

Christ, she was lovely!

Siriol's hands came down from the perfect breasts, left them sitting high on Mavis's chest, still roundly firm. And she drew Mavis's legs further apart and, lifting her head from the profusion of black pubic hair, she eased several fingers inside. Mavis's moans became stronger and she opened those heavenly eyes and uttered a groan as if she were in physical pain. But she was smiling and she straightened up from the waist and lent forward to kiss my best friend on the lips. That made me feel strange. A quiver of something other than sexual curiosity thrilled through me, though we have been so close over the years I can't recall having kissed Siriol on the mouth

132

Cheek to cheek was how we embraced each other in a stylish take-off of the Continental manner. Our friends at school were derisive about our manner of greeting. They said that it was affected and verging on the ridiculous. But we had never expected those philistines to approve or agree with anything we did. It isolated us and only made our fondness for each other grow stronger and more inviolate.

No, I had never kissed Siriol on the mouth. Watching Mavis doing it, so thoroughly and with such competence, made me wonder whether I mightn't learn something from the technique. I had always gone in for a tenderer style of kissing, small feathery touches all over the mouths of my lovers. Tentative probings with the tongue as a prelude to sliding it right inside. The same as my method of fellatio. Zeus Bowen was much enamoured of this approach, saying it was like being ravaged by a highly-sexed Angora rabbit. It goes without saying that I would vary the pressure according to the temperature of the passion gauge. I've never restricted myself to sensitive nibbling, I go in for tempestuous smackeroos of the gob-stopping variety too! But this kissing of Mavis's was different. So workmanlike. Using her tongue as if it were a penis, thrusting it in and out of Siriol's open mouth, proper insertion and withdrawal stuff. I should have thought it was driving Siriol insane.

It was certainly affecting me.

I do get a buzz from erotica, visual and written. It's my opinion that females are more aroused by so-called pornography than Masters and Johnson would have us believe. The reason many women claim that they fail to become excited by seeing pictures of naked bodies sexually cavorting, or fornicating on film, is because they have been programmed to this reaction. It's the prudish inheritance of puritanical Victorian repression. Interesting that girls of my generation, such as Siriol and me, will avidly read magazines aimed specifically at males. We really enjoy them, seeing other girls in the nude. My bedroom might be mistaken for an army barrack room, there are so many female nude pin-ups. I tear them from magazines like *Men Only* and *Playboy*. Mind you, I have male nudes up there too. I don't practise sexual discrimination. Nor do I agree with the feminist claim that these magazines are sexist, that the models are being degraded by the purpose to which their nudity is being put. As wanking fodder. I don't view this as exploitation, that's to take a falsely moral position. Rather, a celebration of the human form, is how I choose to see it. I would have no hesitation in posing if asked. Should I find myself short of cash as a student, which I undoubtedly will, I'll take myself off to the offices of one of those magazines. I don't doubt that they'll be interested, despite my lack of tit. Not all of those girls are built like Chesty Morgan. There's one up on my wall with even less than me! Eva from Sweden, that's who she is, next to Karen from Denmark. My name will look more interesting on the printed page. Boadicea from Bleddwyn-on-Sea. Blodwen (and Mrs Pugh) will have a fit.

It will be good fun, make a field day for future historians when they're researching my background. By then there will be a more liberal view taken of prime ministers posing in the nude. There'll probably be whole calendars of cabinet ministers minus their drawers, a different one for each month. And I might end up as a calendar girl myself. I sincerely hope that they don't make me Ms December, I disapprove of the disgraceful celebration of the birth of that clown, Jesus. The greatest masochist in the history of the human race! Neither would I relish the drizzly month of April. I suppose Ms May would be best. I can see that a coy copywriter might go mad making ghastly puns on the lines of Ms May – or May Not? Never mind.

I was aroused by watching Mavis and Siriol making love. Something held me back from making my presence apparent to them and joining in. This was what I wanted to do more than anything. Afterwards, when I told Boyo about it, he said that I should have. I didn't know whether to be pleased at his openness, at his lack of sexual strictures, or disappointed that he didn't mind sharing me. These thoughts are those of a person in love. The same possessiveness which had plagued me with Zeus Bowen. I must be careful not to suffocate Boyo. Squeeze him to death with my obsessive need to have him all to myself. I'd be hopeless at husband-swapping parties. Unless I were married to a dud, and my big brother were someone else's husband. Then I'd be keen as hot mustard! It was a shame that Boyo was out at the time of my being so aroused. If he'd been in I would have eaten him alive. As it was I had to make do with myself. Myself and a cucumber from the kitchen.

I had never been forced to fall back on vegetables before. After seeing a blue movie featuring fruit I had always intended giving it a whirl. The film starred a young Japanese housewife, married to a sailor, who was away at sea. It was a bunch of bananas that she'd chosen to relieve her sexual frustration. The entire bunch, seven in all. She used one up a day, marking on a calendar the day of her husband's return. The closing shot, symbolically, was of the empty fruit bowl, following a close-up of her full cunt. Full with her handsome husband's cock instead of the brown-speckled skin of ripe banana. Interesting that, not peeling them first. I supposed it was because she wouldn't have easily been able to scoop out minced banana flesh. You'd need another person to lick it all clean, and then no tongue, however long, licks the entire length of the vagina. You'd require an animal like an elephant for that job, making use of his trunk as a sweep cleans a chimney.

My cucumber made no mess whatsoever. The cleanest and coolest screwing device one could find. I shall never hear 'cool as a cucumber' again without entertaining lewd thoughts.

I entertained myself with it in front of the mirror in my bedroom, making certain to lock the door first! It amazed me that Mavis and Siriol could have been so careless with their own door. I can only think that the lust came on them out of the blue, just like that. So that they had no thought in their heads beside having each other there and then. Zeus Bowen and I used to be like that sometimes, in the very early times. Thinking about it, perhaps there had been signs that things were not right before he had taken off for the States. Despite his passionate protestations of devotion I used to see a strangely shifty look in his face, as if he was longing to say something but couldn't bring himself to. Was he trying to break it off with me then?

My mind lingered only briefly on Zeus Bowen as I seated myself at the mirror with my cucumber. He would have enjoyed this, I thought to myself. And I laughed out loud at my reflection. I hadn't undressed. I was too impatient to satiate myself to bother with taking off clothes. I was wearing a skirt, a circle of peach zig-zags that lifted up easily above my hips. I wanted to get a good view of this, every angle in the mirror. I shut my eyes to conjure up again the image of Siriol's fingers in Mavis's cunt. And as it came to me I gradually eased my cuke into my aching twat. God! It was wonderful. Thicker than a cock, even Boyo's. And easier to insert. Like popping a lead pencil into a pursed mouth. The scorching flesh of my fanny really welcomed the coldness. Somehow grasped onto it in a way that was totally unlike having the hot gristle of cock. There was no response from this vegetable, that was one of the differences. When it came time to withdraw it, the cucumber would remain unchanged except for a faint aroma of fish (I must remember to swill it before putting it back in the kitchen – it's sardine salad for the guests this evening). It appealed to me, this gaining satisfaction from an unfeeling and inanimate object. A nice change to be without emotional complications.

Towards the end, as I felt myself approaching a final orgasm (I must have had I don't know how many already!), I heard the telephone ringing downstairs. Well, I wasn't going to answer it, that was for sure. Not with this cucumber coquettishly concealed between my legs. Even with my circular skirt pulled down, with me standing up, the thing still poked out in front – my surrogate penis. How embarrassing it must be for rampant males, caught unawares. Let the telephone answer itself.

Then the ringing stopped, which meant that either Mavis or Siriol must have answered it, or else the caller had rung off. Not very likely, it didn't ring for long enough. And now somebody was calling my name. I recognised the voice, one of the guests. A decent but thoroughly dull bore from Birmingham, who arrives every summer, same week every year with

136

his wife. Then takes it upon himself to do small tasks around the place, all day long, whilst his poor wife has to go and sit on the beach by herself. His current chore was seeing to the sash-cord of the top bathroom window. There was nothing the matter with it until he started meddling. But now the window is jammed, it will neither close nor open any further. Other guests on that floor are complaining bitterly of the draught when they take their baths. Last year he took the door of his bedroom completely off its hinges, claiming that it hadn't been set in correctly when the house was built. He and his wife had been forced to sleep for five of their seven days with no door to their room at all. Just a blanket which Blodwen tacked up over the opening to give them some privacy. We'd had to get in an expert to see to the damage. Blodwen was not going to be pleased about the bathroom window.

'Miss Jones. Miss Jones.' His silly voice floated up the stairs. He's been calling me Miss Jones since I was about nine, the nincompoop. It's his idea of familiarity tempered with bantering formality. I shut my eyes tightly, I was just on the brink, I wasn't going to allow this mutant to spoil my moment of pleasure. Squeezing my thighs as closely together as I could around the cucumber, I pressed it hard against my clitoris. At the same time working my hips in a rotating action. The firm flesh of the vegetable, with just a hint of the softness that surrenders to the teeth, was perfect. Riding faster and faster, I opened my eyes to watch myself in the mirror. It was a stranger staring back at me. A distorted face. Not my own, but somebody more beautiful than I could ever be. Sensual and wild, swollen lipped, with eyes as shiny and sly as a cat's.

I pressed on. As the call for 'Miss Jones' continued, I opened and closed my legs swiftly in a final spasm. And shuddering, I shouted as loudly as I could.

'I'm coming ... I'm coming ... I'm coming ...'

Chapter 17

I am getting ready to go and have tea with Mrs Dilys Bowen, the wife of my ex-lover Zeus. It's difficult to decide what to wear, how to appear, what sort of impression to make. I must have changed as many as four or five times. Siriol can't understand what is taking so long, or why I seem to think it important what I have on.

'You've known each other for years, after all, Bo!' She's bewildered.

I must be careful or she'll begin to suspect that there is more to this than there appears on the surface. But Siriol has little interest in my tea-time outing. Zeus Bowen is still away so the event holds no appeal for her. I have to admit that it doesn't hold very much attraction for me, but it was difficult to refuse her on the telephone. I was in such a relaxed and merry state of mind following my cucumber injection that I would have agreed to anything. And my curiosity overcame any serious doubts that I may have entertained about going.

But now I am filled with a sort of dread and trepidation. The visit has about it the oppressive sense of being a duty-call. As if to an aged aunt, or one of my school-mistresses. And what is the purpose behind it?

'Why has she asked you, d'you suppose?' Siriol is glancing

through the scattered papers on the top of my desk. I have started to clear out my belongings, throw stuff away, in readiness for my departure. The day after tomorrow it will be my eighteenth birthday. I wonder if Blodwen will return for the event?

'I suppose just to be nice,' I say vaguely. Poor old Siriol is beginning to get on my nerves, hanging around here whilst I'm trying to get ready. 'Where's Mavis, then?' These two are seldom apart, I rarely see one without the other. Yet they are tremendously vague and drippy about any kind of future together. If I were them I'd be organising things by now, it's pretty obvious that they're not going to split up, at least not for some while. But things in this house are in limbo, nothing settled, nothing decided, no plan of action. Just a dreary routine of serving three meals a day to these dopes in the dining room. Still, it's almost the end of the season. I suppose it's with Blodwen being away, and Mrs Pugh not being around any longer. That's what it is. But resolving the situation, that will have to wait. I have too many personal problems to think about first. Namely Boyo and me.

'Mavis is out,' Siriol says flatly. I look up at the sound of that voice.

'What's the matter – have you two had a lover's tiff?' I am stripping again, deciding against a demure, grannyish dress, with a creamy lace collar, in favour of a pair of jungle-print Bermuda shorts. I balance some orange plastic sun-specs on the end of my nose and study Siriol earnestly over them.

'That looks nice,' she says. 'I'd wear those.' She has ignored my question.

'Have you two quarrelled,' I repeat the question, 'Siriol?'

She looks out of the window, her finger tracing the splash of seagull shit on the other side of the glass.

'This looks like a tree from the Petrified Forest. Yes, we've had a bit of a tiff if you must know.'

'There's no "if you must know" about it, Siriol. It's obvious that you're busting a gut to tell me.' I glance at my wristwatch, the strap of which I shall have to change if I'm to wear it with these sunglasses and Bermudas. I have the perfect lemon-yellow patent-leather watch-strap to go with this outfit. Already I look the most ghastly eyesore, Dilys Bowen will loathe what I'm wearing. To please her I should be decked out like one of the flower-power children of the sixties, a drippy hippy. I am beginning to feel better about going. The mood of inertia in this house had begun to get me down, I'm a person who believes in positive action. This latest news of the ruffled water between Siriol and Mavis has helped to break the tedium.

'But don't take too long. I've got to be there in half an hour and it'll take me that to stroll over in a leisurely fashion. I don't want to get there sweating like a pig because I've had to run all the way.' I sit down, with my watch-strap ready to change in my hand, the lemon clashing violently with the riot of colour covering my lap. Then I look up expectantly at my friend. She swallows hard. I realise that she is more upset than I thought. She begins to speak in a hollow voice, which might just break into tears. I have no handkerchief to pass over if this should happen. But we two are past the stage of these small politenesses.

'She had a letter from her this morning.'

'I wait, silent and encouraging. When human beings are under stress, their speech suffers immediately. So I leave Siriol to struggle on as best she can.

'It's not the first either. I recognise the writing.' I nod intelligently. 'She's been having them all the time that she and I have been together. They are writing to each other, you see. I think that she's gone out to telephone her now from a telephone box somewhere. So that I can't hear what they're saying to each other. That lousy bitch!' My friend is shouting now and tears are beginning to trickle down her cheek.

'Who's a lousy bitch? Mavis?' I speak calmly, but with sympathy. The big hand on my watch is racing on.

'That old flatmate of hers, that bitch she was living with!'

'Of course,' I say soothingly. '*That* lousy bitch.'

'She's trying to get Mavis back again, this is the point. She says that they are made for each other, that she's in love with Mavis and always will be.'

140

'How do you know? Has Mavis told you all this?' It's getting juicy now. So what if I do arrive at Dilys Bowen's house sweating like a wart-hog – this is getting too good to miss!

'I read this morning's letter. I found it hidden in Mavis's handbag.'

'You went through her handbag – gosh!' I lapse into schoolgirlish (slang) language in my admiration. I admire people who go through other people's possessions. Siriol used to be so sniffy about it at one time, when she discovered me doing the same thing. It was when I stole from our form-mistress's attaché case. I can't remember the full details now, it was so long ago. But I think that Siriol threatened to expose me – she'd had a crush on this teacher at the time. But she didn't, she kept silent. We, the entire class, were punished for my small prank, instead. That was most fun of all – listening to the resentful reaction of all the others to what they regarded as a monstrous injustice. I think that Siriol's respect for me actually took root from that incident. What was it I stole? It can't have been money, that has never attracted me. I believe it was a photograph of a loved one, a fiancé who had been killed in the war. How Freudian if it had been a photograph of the woman's dead mother. There are few photographs of my dead mother in our house. Blodwen has the only one of any clarity.

Siriol is working herself up into a state. I must calm her, the disadvantage of this bedroom of mine is that it is rather too close to other bedrooms for self-expression. This is why I've taken to sneaking into Boyo's bed instead of inviting him into mine. At this time of the year with so many guests still occupying the house, we could easily have been discovered at any time. Zeus Bowen and I were forced to take to the sand-dunes in the summer for this reason. I must keep an eye on the time if I'm to get to his wife on time. Is Dilys plotting to confront me with the past?

'Sh, sh, Siriol.' She has started snivelling, like a young child. The tears are welling up in the green eyes and as quickly are spilling over the lower lashes until they come to a splashing halt on the upper slopes of her bodice. She looks like a

141

young milk-maid today, wearing something rather fearful in fawn cheesecloth. But now is not the time to give her this dispiriting piece of sartorial criticism. I am going to have to run all the way to my tea.

'I had to, Bo. I had to know who this morning's letter was from. She was so different towards me after she'd read it, you see. I could tell right away that it was from the same person because of the writing. The lousy bitch wants her to go back right away – for her birthday.'

'But that's in three days' time! The day after mine!' I am so aghast I'm forgetting that it's Siriol who has been doing such a splendid job in arranging our beach party celebrations.

'I know!' Now she's wailing, throwing herself onto the bed. Spreading snot all over my clothing.

'Oh, don't, Siriol ... don't upset yourself. She won't go, I'm sure she won't.' As I say it, I have a shiver of doubt.

This strange summer, so divorced from reality, so different from all the other summers of my childhood, is drawing to an end. It is inevitable, I have always known it, that Boyo and myself should finish. Perhaps I am better equipped to cope with the sadness of the situation than he is. My real pain come earlier with Zeus, I shan't be able to feel as badly as that for a long time. But Boyo talks wildly of taking off somewhere together. To America, to anywhere that people won't know us. Won't ever guess at our true relationship.

'We can get away with it,' he urges, his face bright with plans. 'We don't look anything alike, after all. It's not as if it were Mavis and me, is it? I can get work, Saul is always at me to try my luck in California with him.' He holds me tightly when we talk of these things. I can imagine Saul Polanski's re-action to me accompanying Boyo to California! Though I was not *compos mentis* on the day of his departure, he didn't visit me to wish me farewell. Nothing like that. And to think that I'd fallen so violently in love with him at first sight! That shows not to trust these bolts from the blue, those heart-pounding moments when the whole world spins around. So much for corny old song lyrics. But I see now that Saul Polanski pointed me in the right direction. He helped in the dethawing process of my heart. So did Ursula. I might not have been so ready for Boyo had those two not broken the ground after the depths I had fallen into after Zeus.

Zeus Bowen – Mrs Bowen. I look at my watch. 'Oh dear, Siriol,' I say it with true regret because there are still lots of things I would have liked to have asked about her and Mavis. I have a feeling that my gorgeous sister may have gone, not just out to the telephone kiosk, but to the station to enquire about trains to Bristol. She had grown increasingly subdued over the plans for the party. She wants it to be more spontaneous, more spur of the moment, than it is turning out. She has hardly asked any of her old pals, claiming that she's gone off them. That the only person she wants to have will be there anyway. Namely Siriol. Yes. Siriol will certainly be there. Probably on her own. But I don't tell her that because I'm about to make a quick getaway. What I do instead is go to my drinks shelf and pour Siriol a stiff whisky, handing it to her neat. No water or soda.

'Get that down you!' I command. She takes the drink from me. 'This is new, isn't it?' I glance at the contents of the bottle. 'New last week,' I comment in what I mean to be a wry voice. There is barely any whisky left at all.

'The shelf of bottles, I mean,' she draws a shuddering breath. This fresh topic is taking her mind off Mavis.

'Ah,' I nod vigorously, nearly dropping my orange sunglasses. Just a scarlet slash across my lips and I'll be ready to go. 'Boyo's demands. He can't relax without something at the ready. Come to think of it perhaps a stiff drink is just what I can do with at this premise mo!' And I peruse my supplies. 'What shall I sample? – may as well finish off this Grand Marnier. Old Dilys will think that I've been eating an orange if she gets close enough for a whiff of the breath. And I laugh out loud at the thought, coaxing Siriol to join me as I do so. Then her eyes fill up with tears again.

'That's it, Siriol, stay here and have a good old weep. And pour yourself another drink, do. I shan't be long, honestly, but I think I ought to go now . . .'

But at that she really seems to break down completely,

throwing her full length along my bed, knocking her drink straight into my pillow. It is immediately obvious that I shall have to throw the pillow away. That or become intoxicated by the fumes each night I lay my head upon it to go to sleep. I must telephone Dilys Bowen to warn her that, not only am I going to be terribly late, but that I might not be able to put in any sort of appearance at all.

I have a crisis on my hands.

When she answers the call the voice sounds so unlike Mrs Dilys Bowen that I think that I must have mis-dialled.

'Sorry, I'm sorry,' I say. 'I must have the wrong number. I'll dial again.' And I almost replace the receiver, but then she speaks again.

'Boadicea? Is that you Boadicea?'

'It is, Mrs Bowen ... I ... I didn't recognise you a minute ago.'

She gave a harshly bright laugh. 'It's the new me.'

'Ah ... well, the thing is that I have a sort of crisis on my hands here. Which means that I'm going to be a bit late. Or,' I hesitate before plunging on, 'do you think we could perhaps make it another day? If it's all the same to you I would much rather do that ...' I trail off into the silence that she's leaving me.

'Mrs Bowen?'

Her reply, when it came, was more determined that I had expected. Harder to refuse. 'I'd much prefer it if we keep to the original plan, my dear. I have made various arrangements so that we shall be able to have a nice quiet chat on our own. The children are all being seen to. I don't need to remind you how intrusive they can be!'

'No,' I say weakly. 'Well in that case if you'll bear with me, then I shall be around as fast as I can.'

'I'll see you then, Boadicea.' There is a pause that seems so deliberate and heavy with insinuated meaning that I find myself unable to replace the receiver and hang on until she puts hers down first. When she does, I lay mine back on its perch. My knees have turned into a pair of poached eggs. They will never support me back up the stairs to tell Siriol that I'm going to have to desert her. I'm certain that the reason Dilys Bowen wants to see me is because she has found out about her husband and me. Why am I feeling this afraid!

By the time I have reached the front door of the Bowen residence, a low and rambling farmhouse on the edge of Bleddwyn Fields, I have managed to rationalise my fears somewhat. I refused to run all this way. I have taken my time, so that now I'm arriving a full hour later than originally planned. My stomach heaves at the prospect of cramming food into my nerve-ridden system. I wonder whether my hostess has any heroin on hand, to be taken intravenously!

When she opens the door I have that same shock of surprise that I had when I saw her that day in Williams's Dairy. Except this time she is looking even better. She is dressed in a rich chrysanthemum bronze smock of soft woven wool. A rough, bobbly material that must seem very pleasing to the touch. It fills out the previously depressing hollows in her figure, and turns her into someone appealingly feminine. Something that she's never been before. Around her neck she is wearing a looping rope of amber stones. Though the effect of these against the woollen smock is just a little too rustic for my callow taste, I can see that many would find the whole spectacle highly fetching. Zeus Bowen, for instance? Their marriage must be going bloody well for a change if his wife has undergone this transformation. Sod it! Sod the shitty marriage! Sod her and particularly sod poxy him!

I smile a blazing smile, one of my brilliant best. My eyes are as cold as a corpse. 'Hello, Mrs Bowen. Sorry I'm so late.'

She comes out on to the curving stone step and leans forward to kiss me. Kiss me! Get her! Leaning against me with one soft cheek against mine, so as not to disturb her lipstick (oh yes, she is painted up like a whore), I could plunge my teeth into her ear-lobe and bite it clean through. Disfigure her for life. So that she won't ever be able to wear a full set of earrings ever again. 'Just one of the pair will do me,' she'll have to explain at the jewellers. 'They are wearing them singly these days.' Cow!

'Boadicea, how lovely to see you. What a wonderful splash

of colour you make in your gay clothes. The children will have been sorry to miss you. I shall have to describe those incredible shorts to them in detail.'

'They are called Bermudas.' I tell her. My smile does not betray the sourness I'm feeling towards her for being able to talk of her children. The children given to her by *my* lover. He must have had to shut his eyes tight when he went through the motions with her, that's for sure. Shut them so bloody tight they must have nearly have been squeezed out through his ear-holes with the pressure.

She smiles back at me. 'Yes. Bermudas. They used to have them in my day too, people in Britain associated Bermudas with crass American tourists. We used to laugh at them in the streets of London. Hardly sophisticated of us was it? Or very hospitable come to that. But come in, Boadicea, this isn't very hospitable of me either. I've got the kettle on, I'm dying for a cup myself, aren't you? Or,' she turns back to me in the hallway, a harmonious background to the colours that she's wearing, 'would something rather stronger suit you more now? You've reached the age where I'm permitted to ask you that now, I'm sure.'

I struggle to answer. Why the hell is she being so bloody nice to me? What is all this smarm leading up to? But I allow none of this to show through my jaunty façade. Instead I swagger behind her, throwing my hips forward in a fashion model's slope. The way I've watched them do on the television. I've often been told that I should consider taking up modelling as a career, because of my tremendous legs and the narrowness of my frame. But this has been from folk who frankly have no idea of my thrusting intellect. They don't know what a fearful waste it would be.

Dilys Bowen knows all right. 'If I didn't know what academic distinctions lie ahead of you, Boadicea,' she is watching me as I move along the hallway, 'I would have said that you could have a successful career in modelling. There's something splendid about the way you have started to wear your clothes. I noticed when we last bumped into each other.'

'I thought the same about you, Mrs Bowen,' I am amazed

to hear myself saying. 'How nice you are looking these days.'

What the hell am I playing at? Am I trying to soften this bitch up before she atempts to annihilate me?

We are entering the low, wooden-beamed ceiling of the long kitchen. It's a lovely room if you like the sort of thing that you see in home decorating magazines. I don't. My tastes run to starker decor, ambiances that resemble factory floors with the workings very much in evidence, 'High Tech' as it is called. If I had my way all telephones and television sets and washing machines would be transparent. Instead of being concealed by opaque coverings. I plan to visit the Pompidou Centre in Paris as soon as I can organise it. The last buildings that I'd care to tour would be St Paul's Cathedral or the Houses of Parliament. I abhor places that are steeped in history and tradition. It depresses me to have to reflect on the past. It's something that I'm going to have to re-think if I'm to assume the leadership of this country from Westminster. I may have to reorganise the entire structure. Arrange it so that the Commons convene in a more modern edifice, like an inflatable Buckminster Fuller Dome on Clapham Common, say. The sort used by circuses. Politics are an extension of the circus, after all. I think it would be appropriate to do away with the false solemnity that is being engendered up to the present time. Perhaps up at Oxford I shall encounter a superior approach to these issues. For the first time in my life I shall be amongst my equals.

The table is laid for tea, I see. The chocolate cake which had always been the speciality of this house – I recall from my baby-sitting days here when I once gobbled an entire cake – is occupying pride of place. Beside it is an earthenware jug containing a trailing profusion of wild flowers. The picture of domestic harmony with the warm bricks of the walls, blending with the orange tiled floor and the brilliant yellow of the paintwork against the ochre curtains at the windows. A place where a man would gratefully hang his hat.

That bastard.

Mrs Dilys Bowen hasn't acknowledged my compliment, she has gone over to the scrubbed pine Welsh dresser against the far wall. There are rows of fine pottery artistically arranged across its surface. Pewter vases containing dried golden leaves. Wide, shallow bowls with gourds overflowing from them. A conglomeration of objects such as stones, pebbles, shells, all chosen for their delicate hues and pale tints. The bleached skeleton-head of a dead sheep. The faint fossil of a fern against the deep purple of a piece of slate. All reminders that the mistress of the house was previously a teacher of art before this marriage. Since then she has not practised her craft at all. Four children, so she claims, has put paid to that. Women manage to have children and continue in their chosen careers these days, I think scornfully. What she has turned into a full-time job, is being the professional wife of the sodding poet.

'A glass of wine, Boadicea. What about that? Which would you prefer? Red, white or rosé? I have all three,' she is smiling encouragingly at me. The lower door of the Welsh dresser conceals a small refrigerator chilling half-bottles of white and rosé wine. Beside the wall next to it is an extensive wine-rack, exceedingly well-stocked with bottles of red, their ruby glow highlighted by a shaft of afternoon sunlight streaming through the window above.

All this is new, and as different in affluence as the changed appearance of Dilys herself. Zeus Bowen's trip to the States must have been extremely successful – and lucrative. Which had never struck me before. Money hadn't been one of our preoccupations when we were together. It was strange to consider Zeus as a wealthy man. But here I am witnessing the first manifestations of money. It only serves to further my scorn.

I say: 'Ah, that'll be lovely, Mrs Bowen. White, please.' I have to think which colour would most comfortably lie alongside that potent swig of Grand Marnier that I gulped before leaving poor Siriol. But already I can taste the icy chill of the white wine cutting through Mrs Bowen's chocolate fudge topping on that inviting cake. There is still some of the greedy child lurking beneath the surface.

'I'll join you.' My hostess withdraws from the refrigerator

with a half-bottle in her hand. 'We'll start with this one, I think. Don't think I'm being mean opening just the half first. You are welcome to drink me dry. It's just that with Zeus away so much and me on my own I find it wiser to order for myself just in halves, otherwise I would get plastered every evening downing a full bottle to myself. I'm not the sort of person who can leave anything once it's been started. I'm the same with boxes of chocolates. I mean to have just the one, and then I make a pig of myself with the lot. All in one sitting.'

'Oh I'm like that too.' I say it so quickly that she laughs.

'Good. That's something that we have in common then.'

Not the only thing, I think.

'Not the only thing though.' She has echoed my exact thought! Jesus! I force myself not to squirm. 'But we'll get onto that in a moment,' she continues, 'first let me absolve my responsibilities as a host.' She is pouring the wine into two thick, large, beautifully-shaped goblets. The liquid is the colour of urine. She raises hers into the air before clinking both our glasses together. 'Here's to the future. Your future, Boadicea.'

'And yours, Mrs Bowen.' My own toast sounds lame and shamefully insincere, but she appears not to notice. Instead she nods her head, the curtains of smooth hair swinging lightly against each cheek. She must not have been as bad as I'd always imagined in her youth. There is a look of today's Blodwen about those bones.

'Yes, all right. And mine. And my future, why not!' And she clinks the two glasses together once again. There is an undertow of recklessness there.

'Now, Boadicea – a slice of cake? Yes?' She laughs easily. 'I thought I'd be able to tempt you with this. Do you remember years ago when you were baby-sitting that time?'

'And I polished one off on my own? I do.' I reply, my agitation is subsiding. This can't be the lead-in to an unpleasant scene. 'That was your fault though, Mrs Bowen, if you had only left me one or two pieces that's all I would have needed.' But she has placed her hand on my arm.

149

'Don't,' I look at her, on my guard again. 'Don't call me Mrs Bowen any more. It must be Dilys from now on. Please. We are able to be on first-name terms, aren't we now, Boadicea?' She is staring at me now, straight into the eyes.

'Yes, Dilys.' I reply, almost mesmerised by her insistence upon this familiarity. If she asked me now whether or not I fucked her husband behind her trusting back I would have to answer honestly, 'yes'.

'Good. Now come, let's settle ourselves shall we? Will we sit at the table or here on the sofa? This way we'll bask in the last of the sun. The sofa I think. You take that end, Boadicea, and I'll take this. I like to rest my weary old legs on this foot-rest. It's pretty isn't it?' She points at the small padded stool, at the crimson rose embroidered on its surface. 'I picked it up in an auction, part of a job-lot with some silver cutlery.'

'Oh.' I answer politely. This kind of talk bores me. Other people's bargains, particularly when they are household objects, hold no fascination for me.

'But I won't bore you with that sort of talk, Boadicea. At your age you can't possibly be interested in household bargains.'

My skin thickens with a blush, I bite avidly into my slice of cake to disguise my embarrassment as greed. But Dilys is not looking at me. She isn't eating cake herself.

'Aren't you having any cake?' I say. It is on trivialities such at this that problems can be kept at bay, enquiries as to people's health, and talk of weather and pets and children. I can ask after the children next.

'Oh no, not for me! I am starting in my middle age to develop that fearful condition known as middle-aged spread. Yes really! And I hate it too, very ageing! Though I have enjoyed leanness all my life – I was like you when I was young, always slim – I now find that I have to be careful.'

This is boring again.

'But one thing that I'm learning is that I mustn't bore people with talk of weight problems. Now that we're settled here I think that we should get on with the point of this meeting, Boadicea. Or rather *I* should get on with it since it was me who rather peremptorily summoned you here. Although it has always been a pleasure to see you, even when you were a small child I sensed the keen intelligence in you. It comes across, maybe not to every one who meets you. But certainly to anyone who has been a teacher. How few I remember with this special quality. None in the classes that I taught alas! But I must get back to the point.' At last! 'The point, the reason I've asked you here today Boadicea – I'll be blunt – is to discuss my husband in his absence. And I do so without any intended disloyalty. It just is more diplomatic to do it this way.'

My heart has risen to meet the chocolate cake on its way down. I pray that the two are going to get on, otherwise I'm going to make a spectacular splash on this sofa. I don't want to at all but I'm staring into her eyes, a completely captive audience. The guilty party. And I'm about to blurt out how sorry I am over the years of infidelity that I shared with her husband. I have already opened my mouth to start saying this but she is lifting a hand to silence me.

'No, let me finish. It won't take long, but it's best to bring this business out into the open now, considering the changed circumstances.'

Changed circumstances! Shit – she knows everything! That it's all over between her husband and me. Every sodding thing. Had she been spying on us that last day in the sanddunes? Crouching on all fours watching her husband cuckold her with me? Or rather, *not* cuckolding her. The memory of his limp dick sprang unbidden into my mind. Bloody thing.

'I am assuming, Boadicea, that the rest of the family know nothing of this affair with my husband?'

Mouth dry, I shake my head. Tantamount to actually confessing.

'I thought not. But you have always been such a clever child, you must have been aware of why Zeus has been such a constant visitor to your house all these years.'

I nod numbly, though it seems to be a particularly banal statement. If I didn't know why her husband spent so much time with me, who in bloody hell would?

'You never discussed it with Blodwen, the subject of Zeus?'

'Never, Mrs Bowen.' I shake my head vehemently. 'Why would I do so?'

She smiles at me gently. 'You're like me, Boadicea. I'm a great believer in the rights of the human animal to personal privacy. But with the state of Blodwen's health being such as it is now I really do think that you should talk to her about it. You see the thing is, the important thing is that I really don't mind any more. I really don't.'

I'm staring at her. There is a lump forming in my throat I'm so moved by her calm acceptance. She laughs softly.

'Don't look at me with those big eyes, Boadicea. You must understand that for many years Zeus and I enjoyed a close and loving relationship and for that I shall always be grateful. I still love him, I always have and I always shall. And I think that he will continue to love me in his own way. But we are no longer necessary to each other. The physical side of our marriage, I know that I can talk to you like this without any embarrassment, the sexual side has been non-active for a long time. It didn't seem an essential any more.'

So he hadn't been lying about that. Not that I ever doubted him.

'But now,' she is glancing down into her drink and lifting the glass to her lips. A soft blush rises up from her neck. For a moment she looks about sixteen. An innocent girl again. 'But now I feel that I am ready to have an affair with someone.'

'Anyone in mind?' The question pops out before I can stop it. Bold and insulting. 'Sorry,' I say, confused, 'I didn't mean that as it sounds.'

But she doesn't mind at all, she hasn't taken offence. Even so she is not letting on. 'My earlier pronouncements about privacy must apply here, Boadicea. You, above all, will understand this.'

I nod humbly and look suitably chastened. It's not what I'm feeling. I have never felt chastened in my life and certainly don't intend to start now. Not in a situation such as this. I'm trying to place the turn of surprising events into some sort of perspective, that's what I am actually engrossed in. I mean to say, as far as I can see, this woman is actually offering me her husband on a plate. Telling me that it's all okay. Giving me the go-ahead. Carte blanche and bloody good luck, have a good time. It occurs to me that I should ask how the gentleman in question feels about it. There are two of us involved, it isn't just me on my own.

And I'm trying hard to sort out my own feelings too. Am I pleased? Do I still want Zeus? Haven't my emotions become soured in that direction? Haven't the subsequent developments with Boyo cancelled out my previous lover's place in my heart? Perhaps I am not so eager to release Mrs Dilys Bowen from her marital obligations after all. I can see that she is the sort of woman who must see her husband happy in his love life before she feels she can take a lover of her own without qualms of conscience.

I object to being used in this way.

'Tell me, Mrs Bowen –'

'Dilys, Boadicea.'

'Tell me, Dilys, have you had all this out with Zeus?'

'He doesn't know that you and I are having this chat.'

This is not what I asked. 'I meant does he know that you know about the affair? Do you speak openly of it together?'

She remained silent for a brief second before replying. 'Well, let's put it this way. It isn't openly acknowledged, but is taken for granted. That's how it is between married couples, as you'll find out.'

'Oh, I shall never get married!' I say quickly. She smiles at me in a patronising fashion. 'Not ever.' I'm using my very firm voice. She needn't think that I'm here to pick up her left-overs, just like that. Simply because she doesn't want him any more.

'Well, Boadicea, I understand that point of view. If I were your generation and with your prospects I should feel the same. But I think we are talking about love here, I really do, not marriage. And with Blodwen in her present state, the situation must be resolved. Has to be sooner or later.'

I stare at her, distaste gradually forming in the warmth she'd coaxed from me. Isn't this the woman that I've despised for the past five years? Why am I wasting my time here being told like a child – and that's really how she's addressing me – that I must divulge the remnants of my big love affair to the member of my family that I managed cleverly to keep in the dark for its entire duration?

'I must say that I don't really see why I should have to say anything to Blodwen. I'm leaving Bleddwyn pretty soon to lead my own life and I think that Blodwen must learn to lead hers. We don't depend on each other's approval, you know.'

She nodded. 'I understand that, Boadicea. But I still think that Blodwen warrants more understanding and sympathy than you seem prepared to give. The fact that she has stayed away as long as she has this summer shows that she is deeply self-conscious about her condition.'

'It was only depression.' I say in a stubborn voice streaked with resentment. Blodwen is *my* sister after all, I don't need an outsider to tell me about her state of health or mind. We know, as a family, what's going on in our own ranks for Christ's sake!

'In the earlier weeks, possibly so – that was only natural. It happens to many women at her age and at that stage. But now she has much more on her hands, and she must be taken care of. She needs kindness from those closest to her. And you are surely one of those, Boadicea.'

'You mean that she's worse now?'

'Worse – ah, you mean worse mentally. Well, from my experience of pregnancy I would say that now your sister is over the first three-month hurdle, I should think that she is probably better. And, of course, she has the father of the child close at hand now – again that's always a great help. And Zeus, whatever faults he has, will always be a most marvellous father. He loves children, as you very well know, Boadicea, from your baby-sitting days. Do you remember how he used to try and keep them up as late as he could, even though we were due out? So Blodwen is well blessed in her choice of a man to take care of her during her pregnancy. And he will love their little baby just as well as he loves all ours. And if my

154

plan works out, as I hope it will do, the tiny thing will be brought up alongside the others. All one happy family. This is what I really wanted to talk about to you, Boadicea. What would be your attitude to having an oldster such as myself in your ranks? You see – I've been accepted as a mature student, to do a post-graduate course, starting this September. I'm going to suggest that Blodwen moves in here, in my place, to take care of Zeus and the family. She'll find the children will adapt easily, and they'll be so thrilled with the baby. What do you think, Boadicea?'

'I think . . . I'll have another drink.'

Chapter 18

I am strolling through Leicester Square squinting up at Boyo, who is smiling down at me from above the Odeon cinema. He is in the nude but chastely turned, bunched buttocks to the fore (fifteen years since I fondled those fair globes), and must measure roughly 250 ft high. Which would make his penis . . . I gag at the thought! Then pause to reflect on the magnetism of my brother's image. He is a golden-skinned god towering over the city, the grin as irresistible as when he was a boy. And the adult machismo has strengthened the appeal. He is billed as the sexiest super-stud of all the Hollywood super-stars. It's not hard to see why, studying this hoarding. The extra attraction lies in the arrogant mockery of the eyes. 'This man is a MENACE', the posters scream, 'to women!' Menace, my eye! What a load of codswallop! Boyo has about as much menace in him now as an over-ripe grapefruit, his potency milked out of him by his Svengali, Saul Polanski. But the public wouldn't have any way of knowing that – what the hell. Boyo got what he always wanted, fame and vast fortune. Everything except me.

I make a sharp swerve, leaving Leicester Square behind me, passing the Lesbos Arts Centre which now incorporates the old Comedy Theatre. I see that *Such as Us* is into its third year, with Ursula still in the lead. This is the rôle for which she received the *Edith Evans Award, Muse Italianna* and the *Prix d'Paris International,* and she is expected to be nominated for an Oscar when the film is completed. Fresh photographs have been taken of the production to include the changes of cast in the supporting rôles. In each of them Ursula dominates as ever, her mane of tigerish hair as spectacular as the first time I set eyes on it at the 'No Name' in Cardiff. A club which, alas, has never been resurrected since the explosions of twelve years ago when local political fervour ran so high and so much of that area of dock-land was destroyed.

I resolve (yet again) to arrange a meeting with Ursula one of these days – it could be amusing to re-live old times!

I glance discreetly over my shoulder before continuing towards my destination. Two men have been following me along the street, as they should be. I expect this. One is a short distance behind the other and is slouching close to the wall on the opposite pavement. If I wasn't absolutely certain that he was on my trail I wouldn't even notice him. A nonentity. I smile. These are usually the sort of men that I find sniffing along in my wake.

But the other is rather more distinguished, a man whom one might pick out in a crowd. Attractive. A frown creases my clear brow, but fades as I cross the road towards the newsstand. Being followed by men in the street is a small price to pay for the freedom of being able to stroll around London in this fashion. In some cities it would be absolutely impossible. And the news is increasingly cheerful. I see from the headlines that yet more oil has been discovered in the Bristol Channel. Mavis and Siriol will be pleased. They will probably be planning already to purchase yet another chunk of coastline to build yet another de-luxe hotel. Unless they're in the mood now to think of an early retirement, or start all over again in somewhere like the West Indies. A place where Mavis can spend her days stretched out in the sun, frying herself to a charred cinder, gorging herself on whatever she can get into her mouth, behaving generally like a female Bacchus – whilst still remaining faithful to poor old Siriol. Just! Still together and devoted, after all these years. A fifteen-year-old marriage, they call it. Each year they send me the photographs of their 'wedding anniversary' celebrations, with the staffs of their hotels toasting them with champagne. One year I really must attend one of these festive gatherings. It isn't for want of an invitation – it's just a question of fitting it in.

As I buy an evening newspaper, my eyes are drawn to yet another member of my family, my brother-in-law. His bland, venal features sneer superciliously from the prestigious cover of *Poetry Quarterly*. He is wearing the same suit, navy-blue with a neat waistcoat, that he always wears for his weekly 'Poet's Corner' programme on ITV. His only concession to Bohemia being his pipe, a useful accessory which he uses mainly for tapping his teeth and scratching his bald head. Many impersonators score easy successes with their pipes in imitations of him. So do cartoonists.

Oh yes, Zeus Bowen is enough a figure of the establishment now to be pilloried in this way. The man in the street knows his name. Only those admirers still passionate in their praise of his early work mourn the non-fulfilment of that exceptional promise. For Zeus Bowen has not written a poem in fifteen years. His muse departed then, so it is lamented. My sister Blodwen is no replacement for me.

But now I am almost at my destination. I am recording a short broadcast in the BBC studio in Lower Regent Street. It won't take long, not more than half-an-hour, and my chauffeur will be waiting for me with the Daimler. He disapproves of me wandering the streets as I'm doing now. He sees danger at every turn – the silly boy. He can't begin to understand how precious these short strolls are to me, being just like everyone else. With the sense of street excitement . . .

I glance over my shoulder again. I have arrived at the studio and the commissionaire is bowing slightly and opening the door. But I am looking to see which of my shadows has managed to catch up with me. It's the attractive one. Goody. I turn to face him, and he is even better close-up.

158

'I shall be in here for a while, but I am a little early. Would you care to come with me and wait?' There can be no doubt what my speculative gaze is saying. He replies steadily, his eyes on mine (it's going to be a pleasant interlude).

'Whatever you prefer, Prime Minister.'